BLACK SOIL

Stories by Peter Bishop

Published by Toombul Publishing
millera@bigpond.com

ISBN: 978-0-9872014-0-9

Printed by Hunter Valley Printing
90 Kelly Street, Scone NSW Australia 2337

CONTENTS

The Clock 5

Lukey 25

The English Teacher 39

Fish Beetle 55

Coconuts 66

Mice 72

All Men 75

Liberation 79

Salt Fly 83

High Tide 98

Clarissa...102

Dick and Jane 123

Pension Plan..128

Inez..150

Nullarbor 160

Golden Fields Forever............................173

Global Seaweed 180

The Woodbox 199

To Dinie

Who has put up with a lot.

THE CLOCK

'I'm not having another damn clock in this house.'

There was a finality in Marie's voice that Roger knew was beyond negotiation. 'Susan's teeth need braces – Geoffrey's basketball excursion to New Zealand comes up in May and I'm not putting up with that wretched stove for one more day.'

Marie's granitic phrases echoed in Roger's head as he stood in front of the clock. He should never have mentioned this auction.

The clock was a regulator – taller than his head, accumulated grime of over half a century encrusted upon its every surface – a plain arched top above a twelve inch silvered dial, three delicate black hands – the largest sweeping the entire dial every hour, a small second hand above, a single hour hand below, three dials within the one silvered disk.

Joseph Weinberger, Sydney in black across the centre of the dial.

Below the face delicate mahogany scrollwork, the whole case glazed in three panels, slender mahogany pillars – great mercury-filled pendulum, massive single brass weight.

Roger's scalp prickled.

This was special. He'd never heard of Joseph Weinberger – some Sydney jeweler in the Victorian era perhaps – certainly no Australian clockmaker Roger had ever heard of, and he knew most of them. Weinberger not on the list. It had to be English, early Victorian maybe, but English definitely.

The catalogue estimate was $3000 - $5000.

Roger had no cash.

Well, that wasn't strictly true. There was the investment fund they were setting aside for the kids' tertiary education. $13,000 one way or another – mostly shares.

His money really. Taken from his income, administered by him. Although Marie would say it was her sacrifices that had made the savings possible.

Three to five thousand dollars. It had to be worth more than that.

He'd have to get the dial re-silvered – get rid of all those scratch-marks around the screwholes, preserve the original black figuring. That'd cost five hundred.

The glass was okay – it had the wavy look of original glass – the clock had the air of something which had remained motionless for half a century or more. He had to see the movement.

Roger popped the catch on the glass door – the hinges squealed in protest.

'I'm sorry sir, I can't allow you to open the cabinet.'

Damn.

'I can show you the report of our service horologist sir.'

Probably mid-Victorian, little evidence of Australian manufacture, most likely English. In need of general overhaul. All bearings encrusted with hardened residues. Lubricated generally, freed up main pinion and bearings to allow mechanism to run. Little signs of wear in bearings. Labour $136.00.
D. H. Lawrence, specialist in restructuring time.

Roger had seen a picture of an identical clock on the internet. He found it again that night. Sold three years ago, US$14,500 – identical, even to the mahogany scrollwork. Identical.

Made by E L Simmons, c.1790.

Identical. With Harrison maintaining power and mercury-filled pendulum and beat adjuster.

What if this were its twin? He could restore and sell it for $20,000 – in a flash. The kids' fund would actually make money out of it.

***

'Where have you been Roger? I've been leaving messages at your desk all day – no-one seems to know where you were.'

'Had to take a client to lunch' Roger gave Marie a peck on the cheek.

'Well why didn't your secretary tell me that? – birdbrain that girl – what's her name?'

'Isobel.'

'Isobel, yes, that's her – skirt too short, always patting her hair – why you keep her Roger I'm sure I don't know.'

'Izzy didn't know where I was, I met this bloke in the lobby, he wanted lunch, one thing led to another – it dragged on longer than I expected.

'Well, I hope it was worth while.'

Roger shook his head. 'I dunno, too early to tell.'

'The amount of work you do for that firm – it's time they gave you a raise Roger – you're too timid – you should ask for it – Lord knows we need it.

'John Smifferson told me Susan's teeth are going to need four years treatment to correct her bite. He wants to take out two teeth top and bottom and then bring the remaining teeth in to fill in the gaps.'

'I don't see why he has to take out perfectly good teeth.'

'That's because you're not an orthodontist Roger – you are a marketing consultant – John Smifferson's an orthodontist, and a very good one. If John had something to sell he'd come to you. When we have children with bite problems, we go to him. We owe it to our children to look after their future.'

'It still seems crazy to me – pulling out perfectly good teeth. Nature must think there's room for them or why does she keep producing kids with all those teeth.

'She'd just say whoops! Too many teeth! Have to cut back next time – before you know it orthodontists'd be out of business.'

'You know Roger, sometimes I think you're just as childish as all the rest of those people in that office of yours.

'Unless you want poor Susan to grow up with a smile like a crocodile we have to do something about her bite now, poor little thing, before it's too late.

'It's not as if she wants to wear bands for the next four years – and it's not as if I couldn't do with new clothes now and again – but if we choose to have children we take on all the responsibilities that come with them – and that includes looking after their teeth.'

'Looking after John Smifferson more likely.'

'Roger, I will not hear a word against John Smifferson – he's the perfect family man – he and Joan have five children and she's always on a stall at the school fete, and she helps in chapel – she's a lovely person, and so is he – and so are his children.'

'How are their teeth?'

'Roger, now stop that! I know it's expensive – but we must think of Susan's future. I've spoken to a lot of the mothers in Susan's year and almost half of them have had corrective procedures performed on their children's teeth by John.

'They take it as a matter of course. We can always dip into the children's tertiary fund if we need to – for things like this anyway. And Geoffrey's excursion is really very reasonable – it's only $1500 for the whole two weeks, including the air fare.

'You should be proud of him Roger, even if he is only a reserve. It would be churlish of us not to send him just because he's a reserve. Just imagine what the other parents might think.

'No, my mind's quite made up on this Roger – Susan has her teeth done and Geoffrey goes on his basketball excursion. And don't look at me like that.'

***

Roger's mobile phone rang at 4.17 pm Tuesday.

'Mr Corbett?

'Speaking.'

'Martin, of Dixon's auctions here Mr Corbett. We are at lot C74 in the catalogue Mr Corbett – I understand you are interested in the very fine regulator lot C 76, is that correct?'

Roger's heart quickened. 'Yes Martin.' In the background he could the echoing loudspeakered voice of the auctioneer.

'Excellent, Mr Corbett. They are now dealing with lot C75 – there are three telephone bidders on the line for lot C76 I'm afraid.

'Lot C75 is completed – oh dear, Mr Dixon is now referring to the regulator as the *piece de resistance* of the catalogue –'

Roger could vaguely distinguish the words.

'Yes Mr Corbett – Mr Dixon is now calling for opening bids – do you wish to make an opening bid Mr Corbett?'

'Not yet Martin.'

'Mr Dixon has opened the bidding at five thousand dollars – now six, six point five, seven thousand – do you wish to make a bid Mr Corbett?'

'Not yet Martin.'

Roger's heart was racing, his palms sweating.

'Eight thousand Mr Corbett, from the floor – the telephone bidders are out now, Mr Corbett. Do you wish to make a bid?'

'Not yet, Martin.'

"Eight and one half thousand from the floor – nine thousand – nine thousand – Mr Dixon is calling fair warning Mr Corbett, fair warning.'

'Ten thousand Martin.'

'Ten thousand, thank you Mr Corbett, your bid, ten thousand fair warning, fair warning – oh dear – ten thousand five hundred from the floor Mr Corbett.'

'Eleven thousand Martin.'

'Eleven thousand it is, thank you Mr Corbett, eleven thousand, eleven thousand fair warning – I think we have it Mr Corbett – eleven thousand five hundred from the floor. I'm sorry about that Mr Corbett – the bid is eleven thousand five hundred dollars against us Mr Corbett, eleven thousand five hundred dollars fair warning, do you wish to make another bid Mr Corbett? Mr Dixon is looking at me – eleven thousand five hundred dollars fair warning twice – '

'Twelve thousand, Martin.'

'Twelve thousand Mr Corbett – thank you, twelve thousand it is, twelve thousand fair warning, twelve thousand fair warning twice –

'Sold for twelve thousand dollars Mr Corbett! And congratulations, well purchased! Thank you Mr Corbett.'

Twelve thousand dollars! What had come over him? Roger's hands were trembling as he pushed the disconnect button and laid the phone on his desk.

Twelve thousand dollars! He'd planned to go to six thousand, no more. Twelve thousand – he'd have to sell all the shares in the kids' education fund, he'd be up for 30% capital gains tax – still, that wouldn't be payable till next year – but God! Twelve thousand dollars!

And the buyer's premium! He'd forgotten the buyer's premium! Another 12.5%. That was another $1500. Oh God. Thirteen thousand five hundred dollars all up. He'd get $13,000 for the kids' shares if he was lucky. What had he done?

Roger felt sick in the pit of his stomach – how accurate that phrase was – the pit of his stomach – an entire open-cut coal mine had just started operations there.

Thirteen thousand five hundred dollars – oh God. What was he going to do? He couldn't tell Marie – he just couldn't. The kids' fund had $13,000 tops – less tax it was more like $10,000, but he'd just spent $13,500 – without the extras he'd have to spend on the clock – silvering the dial for a start – god knows what else. He'd have to borrow against something. Maybe the mortgage on the house – there was unencumbered equity in there, but it was in their joint names – Marie'd have to sign anything there. Bankcard would have to carry it.

Still – he had the clock. Roger drove out to the auction rooms at Abbotsford.

'Mr Corbett, I'm Martin. Delighted to meet you in person. Have you come to collect your Regulator?'

'Yes Martin, I'd like to have a look at it first if you don't mind.'

'Of course, Mr Corbett. And if you could then come to the office, we can finalise settlement details.'

'I can only pay $4,000 today Martin – it'll take me some time to sell shares and so on – '

'That will be perfectly alright Mr Corbett – we will be happy to release it to you on $4,000 deposit – how soon will you be able to provide the balance?'

'Two weeks – is that okay?"

'Two weeks will be fine Mr Corbett – not a problem. Now, here it is – lovely thing isn't it?'

The clock looked shabbier than Roger had remembered. There was a blister in the veneer over the arched dome that he hadn't seen before, and a small crack in the bottom corner of the left hand glass panel.

'That's new Martin.'

'What's that Mr Corbett? Oh dear – I see – yes – I can't recall seeing that myself. Such a shame. I don't think you'll have too much trouble re-glazing that panel though – there are glaziers specializing in old glass – I'll give you a name in the office. They're not cheap of course, but very good.'

The gut was unraveling on the weight suspension. Roger hadn't noticed that before. And the beat scale below the pendulum was crooked. There was a moth trapped between the mahogany scrollwork and the glazed door.

***

'Izzy, I wonder if I could ask you for a favour.'

'Well Roger, I won't know until you ask me, – what is it?'

'I've got a clock and I ….'

'A clock!?'

'Yes – a big clock – like a grandfather clock.'

'Good god. Yes, well, go on…'

'Well, I've got this clock and I can't take it home and I was wondering if I could keep it at your place – ?'

'A clock, Roger. A clock.!'

'Yes. I'd need to do some work on it from time to time, but I wouldn't get in your road – I'd only come when it suited you. I remember you saying you had a garage, and you haven't got a car…'

'And what does your wife think of all this?'

'Well that's the point – I can't take it home because I can't tell her about it.'

'Why not? Is it a surprise?'

'Well yes, in a way, you could say it is a surprise alright – yes, you could say that.'

'A clock – well, it's a start I suppose. Okay Roger, you can leave it at my place – how big is it?'

'A bit bigger than me.'

'Okay, well it can go in the garage I suppose.'

'Is it safe there?'

'Oh Roger, it's got a locking door and everything – Jesus, it's only a bloody clock!'

'Thanks Izzy, thanks. It'll be great.'

'A clock. Jesus Roger.'

***

Isobel's garage was big, empty, an overhead light, even a bench and power point at the far end, and a locking steel roll-down door. The first thing Roger did was lay the clock down on the bench, remove the dial and send it off for re-silvering.

He removed the heavy brass works with their thick plates and solid pillars, he took the plates apart, cleaned and polished the heavy drive wheels with their handcarved spokes, their finely cut teeth.

Joseph Weinberger, Sydney, 1821 emerged, an inscription under the verdigris on the back plate. Roger's heart beat a little harder when he discovered that. It was rare for any other than the clockmaker himself to put his name on both the front and the back-plate of a clock.

Roger began to think the clock might be worth $20,000 after all.

Every moment he could, he spent in Isobel's garage, cleaning and restoring the clock. The brass sheathed weight was solid lead, not the lead chips of later clocks. He uncovered the finely engraved ring of a micrometer adjustment above the metal-sheathed jar of the mercury pendulum. It was extremely rare to find the original mercury jar intact. Roger lovingly cleaned and polished every piece.

Roger had other clocks at home, five in fact, some of them ran, some were in pieces – he'd fix them one day – but none of them came anywhere near this one in sheer precision and quality.

At first Isobel had brought cups of coffee and stood by, making conversation as Roger toiled with the intricacies of his clock.

But his replies were disjointed, distracted – and in the end Isobel gave up, walked away, left him to it. Roger didn't notice she was gone.

When he cleaned the bearings they showed little wear, the faces of the teeth hardly altered. Roger took photos, sent them to Christies, Sothebys, horologists in USA and Britain. He polished the case – he wondered about that, but in the end he polished it – gently, with wax and endless patience. No shellac. And under the layers of dirt the mahogany was beautiful – veneered on oak – honeyed golden from the sunlight of centuries. It took him a week to clean the scrollwork.

***

'John Smifferson wants $4000 for removing Susan's teeth Roger.'

'Good God! That's a thousand dollars a tooth!'

'What's done is done, Roger – here's his account. He needed an anaethsthetist and an assistant, so of course it's expensive. And poor little Susan's mouth, it's so sore. We'll just have to sell some shares in the education fund.'

***

'Roger – John Smifferson tells me he hasn't been paid for Susan's extractions. The poor man, he was so embarrassed – and so was I of course – I gave you his account three weeks ago Roger – how could you be so forgetful?

'Really Roger, you must be more responsible about these things, sometimes you act just like a little boy.

'All this extra work you've been doing – I think you're quite forgetting your family. Now make sure you attend to this Roger – really – it's just too embarrassing. And now there's another $1500 for the braces.

'He's done such a wonderful job, you can hardly see them – if you even bother to look at your daughter that is.

'I don't know what's the matter with you Roger – you seem to be living a separate existence these days – if I didn't know you better I'd say you were having an affair.'

***

Roger read the microfiche extracts from the Old Bailey court records of 1802.

Solomon Weinberger, clockmaker apprentice to E L Simmons of Cumberland street London, convicted of fraudulent use of lead in silver castings for his grace, the Earl of Faversham, transported to Australia on the barque Alexandria for seven years.

Clockmaker. Apprenticed to Simmons. Had he taken Simmons drawings? Copied them perhaps? The clock may be worth more than $20,000.

***

Roger opened the bubble-wrapped package. Hammond had re-silvered the twelve inch dial with great delicacy. He'd even re-touched the black numerals and the signature where small pieces had flaked away, all done with such artistry that it was impossible to pick which was restored, which was original.

A small envelope fell from the bubble-wrap.
To restore, re-silver and re-enamel twelve inch regulator dial:
$2,175.00 including GST.
J. K. Hammond.

Two thousand dollars! Roger had allowed $500 for the dial.

But oh god it was beautiful. Roger spent an hour setting the dial in place and re-attaching the hands. He should have had them re-enameled at the same time, they looked a little shabby now. Still, just as well he hadn't. He didn't know how he was going to pay for the dial.

The kids' shares hadn't sold as well as he'd hoped – $11,579 after commissions and stamp duty – that'd be around $9,000 after tax. He could probably squeeze most of it into bankcard this month.

The clock was beautiful. The aged mahogany glowed with

the pale honey bestowed by ancient sunshine and old shop windows. Roger had re-spun the suspension gut by hand, wax and resin bonding the frayed pieces back into the cord. It had worked marvelously.

The pendulum moved in stately fashion across the beat scale, skeins of light sliding up and down polished cylindrical shapes with each measured swing.

***

'Roger, where were you today? I called the office at five to get a lift home and you had already gone. And that twit of a girl of yours, I couldn't get any sense out of her at all.'

'I was out with a client.'

'Well why didn't that stupid Lizzie or Dizzie or whatever her name is say so? Really Roger – that girl is a total fool.'

'She didn't know Marie – she doesn't know everything I do. And she's actually a nice girl, and a good secretary. Besides, she's not just mine, three of us share her.'

'Well, I got the distinct impression that the girl's a fool, or she's covering for you in some way I can't quite comprehend. And if she was, I don't suppose you'd tell me anyhow.

'Don't take any liberties with me Roger – I must say you've been a bit peculiar lately. If you're up to something Roger – I'll find out you know – you can't keep a secret for ten seconds you know.

'Now make sure you send in the deposit for Geoffrey's excursion – it's due in this week – the school wants a thousand dollars, the balance two weeks before they leave.'

***

Roger gazed at the clock – at last completely restored and re-assembled.

It looked superb, the silvered dial hanging above the slender mahogany columns, the second-hand moving with deliberate precision on its meticulous passage around the dial, a small tremor each time the pallets released the escapement.

The time and patience it must have taken old Weinberger – it could have been ten years – every wheel, every spoke, every tooth carefully cut by hand, measured with meticulous precision. Some of the old astrological regulators had been twenty years and more in the building. Weinberger may have easily put ten years of his life into this one.

And Weinberger had cut no corners. All the hubs swaged onto their arbours, wheels screwed to their hubs, the plates holding the drive-work wonderfully thick, bound with no less than five massive pillars – maybe more than ten years.

And the simple elegance of it. Clearly he had copied the Simmons clock, he may well have worked on that himself, copied the drawings. Superb.

Isobel came into the garage.

'Oh Roger, you've finished it, haven't you! I must say it does look beautiful.'

'Thanks Izzy – yes, it's done. I'm sorry in a way that it's over – it is a rather graceful old thing, isn't it?'

Isobel tucked her arm into his.

'Come and have a little celebratory drink – I've got most of the remains of a bottle of brandy upstairs, and I hate drinking alone.'

'Sounds good Izzy – why not? God knows how I'm going to pay for it all.'

'But you've already bought it Roger – it's paid for – I know that because you told me how much it cost.'

'Yes but I haven't paid for Susan's teeth – or her braces, and Geoffrey's excursion – there's six and a half thousand dollars I'm supposed to have paid already – and I just haven't got it.'

'Jesus Rog, you do need a drink. Come on.' Isobel led him up the stairs into her two room unit – three if you counted the bathroom, which it was probably better not to do.

***

When Marie exploded into the room most of the brandy had gone. Roger was sitting on the sofa with Izzy – tearful – telling Izzy more and more of the financial black hole he had dug with the clock – and Izzy – kindhearted, husbandless Izzy – was cradling him against her bosom – and the short skirt had almost given up the battle.

It didn't look too good from the outside, which was where Marie was standing.

'Dammitall Roger – I knew you were up to something, you and this birdbrained little twit – you've been flaunting her in my face all this time Roger, haven't you!? – You both must have had your share of laughs at my expense!'

'Marie – you're totally wrong. There's absolutely nothing between Izzy and me.' Roger sat up and Izzy tugged at her skirt – but it didn't improve things much.

'Don't lie to me Roger – don't lie to me – you've been

spending all our money on this strumpet! This little tart!

'Poor John Smifferson hasn't been paid – the poor man rang me up! The shame of it! And the school – Geoffrey has missed his excursion because you didn't pay the deposit, and here you are spending our money on this…. this creature!'

'Marie don't be ridiculous – I haven't spent a penny on Izzy. I'm only here because Izzy said I could keep the clock here.'

'Clock!? Clock!?' For a microsecond Roger thought Marie sounded like some enormous broody hen – from nowhere a grin surfaced.

'What are you talking about Roger? And what are you smirking at? Have you become feeble minded as well as an adulterer?'

'No Marie, no – none of those things. Come with me and I'll show you.'

Down two dark flight of concrete stairs, Roger opened the blue steel door of the garage and turned on the fluorescent light.

The clock glowed golden honey in the light, pendulum swaying, reflections playing up and down the lovingly polished surfaces.

Marie stood stock still inside the garage.

'What is that, Roger?'

'It's a Regulator – an old Regulator.'

'Where did it come from?'

'I bought it at auction.'

'How much Roger? – how much of our money did you throw away on this piece of junk?'

'Thirteen and a half thousand dollars, and I've spent another three thousand on it since then – so sixteen or seventeen thousand it's cost.'

'Seventeen thousand dollars Roger – for this piece of old rubbish!? Tell me you're joking Roger – please tell me you're joking.'

'It's worth more than seventeen thousand now dear – it's worth more money now that I've done it up.'

'Is it now, Roger? Is it really? Just like those other useless clocks cluttering up our house – I suppose they're worth more money too – is that right Roger?'

'Well, yes dear, they are. But not as much as this one – this one might be worth twenty thousand dollars to the right person.'

'Twenty thousand dollars – to the right person of course – we mustn't overlook the right person now, must we Roger.'

Marie advanced on the clock.

'What about Susan's teeth, Roger? Is she going to grow up deformed because you spent her money on this damned clock!?

'And Geoffrey – excluded from the team – ridiculed by his classmates to say nothing of how the humiliation of it affects me – and all so you can have your stupid clock!'

'Well, I'll show you what I think of your wretched clock Roger – I'll show you how it might look in the hands of the wrong person –' and Marie seized the clock case by the top and hurled the whole thing down onto the concrete floor.

'I'll show you Roger!' and she stamped her substantial feet on the shattered casing, on the splintered scrollwork, on the shards of glass. An errant shard cut her ankle, blood spattered.

'I'll show you how the wrong person might look at this clock of yours Roger' and Marie, panting now, grabbed a hammer from the bench and began beating the silvered face of the clock.

Black hands splintered off, the silver dial buckled, brass cogs and wheels squeezed their way out between distorted plates – the hammer smashed the glass jar of the pendulum and mercury joined the shattered glass and splintered timber, mingled with Marie's blood, the concrete floor quite slippery in spots.

'I'll show you Roger' and Marie hammered at the tangle of brass and silver, small toothed fragments splaying across the floor – 'I'll show you,' sobbing now, the handle of the hammer, slick and slippery, finally sliding from her grasp.

Marie sat heavily in the litter of destruction. A small blade of glass opened a red smile on her thigh, another crimson blossom flowered beneath a buttock.

Roger stood frozen, immobile since that first awful crash.

It was Izzy who helped her up, bathed her wounds, called the ambulance.

Sothebys Fine Arts and Antiquities London,

Friday November 25th 2005.
Mr Roger Corbett,
19 Waterford Drive,
Roselle, NSW, Australia.

Dear Mr Corbett,

Thank you for the excellent photographs of your very fine regulator by Mr Joseph Weinberger.

Clocks of Australian manufacture from this period are extremely rare, as you will well know.

Indeed the only colonial clockmaker of that time who springs readily to mind is Mr Oatley.

Subject to inspection and verification by our people, although from your excellent photographs there can be little doubt of authenticity, we believe we can confidently anticipate a price at auction well in excess of seventy five thousand pounds.

We look forward to acting on your behalf in this matter, and eagerly await your instructions regarding the disposal of this exceptionally fine clock.

With kindest regards, I remain yours faithfully,

John Robertson,
Head of Fine Arts and Antiquities, Sothebys, London, UK.

LUKEY

Lukey Pease had a German Shorthaired called Jazz – a touch of Doberman about the teeth, the eyes, and Jazz had a nose on him could track a goanna up a tree.

Mid morning and Lukey walked, Jazz galloped through the whitetop paddock and Jazz's gallop sank into cold treacle, yellow eyes eager, nose questing – locked upwind, legs stilled mid-stride, body quivering.

Lukey crept forward beside Jazz, silent as a cloud brushing the ground, slowly pulling off his old felt hat. Cat swift he clamped the hat over a sett of brown quail huddled under the whitetop tussock. One burst into the air with an explosive whirr and Jazz watched its flight, eyes full of reproach.

Lukey folded his hat over speckled brown bodies, crept his fingers into the warm fluttering bunch, crushed small skulls, put the quail in his jacket pockets, walked down the hill to the scattering of cottages along the creek.

Mavis Adamson, soft skinned, long hair damp against her forehead, hung washing on the line back of her house. She bent down to the basket, lifted a shirt, mouth full of pegs – there was already heat in the morning sun, and her shift clung, pulled free, clung again.

Mavis wiped dark hair from her face, looked up.

'Lukey – You like to scare me creeping up like that' – but Mavis did not look scared.

The creek took a big sweep below the Adamson house,

round a spur that hid the other houses. Mavis stood there, sunlight making light of her shift.

'Cut some kindling for ya while ya finish that' said Lukey. 'Got me some little quails – ya like quails? I can skin em, wrap em in bacon, push a bit of apple inside em, put in a bit of rosemary if ya like.'

'That sounds real nice Lukey – Dan's down to the sawmill, took his lunch.'

Lukey nodded, lifted the little tomahawk out of the grip of the chopping block, took an offcut of deal, split it into long pale fingers. By the time he'd taken three armfuls to the box by the back door Mavis had the washing pegged and hoisted, pale flags waving in the sunshine.

Mavis held the back door open, smiling at Lukey, a fine dew on her top lip, dress clinging to dampness here and there, a waft like the sweet breath of early morning milkers.

'Home, Jazz,' and the dog's tail drooped and his ears fell and he turned and trotted up the hill, stopped, looked back, and Lukey waved him away, 'Go on now, git,' and the dog turned and trotted out of sight.

***

Lukey's horse Tom was a big old Clydesdale, pulled the sulky when there was things to carry. Tom grazed in the meadow, the sulky rested shafts down in the grass by the cottage – a cottage tucked in a fold of the cliffs out where people seldom came.

Sandstone cliffs grey with lichens bulged above the ironbark and wattle, soft yellow caves like the gills of mushrooms pocked the sides, housed swallows and bats, goannas and jewlizards, possums and skinks, wasps and snakes, handprints in ancient ochre.

A cloud of cockatoos drifted white and raucous against the tall cliffs and their secrets.

Lukey's cottage sat beneath them, walled in old grey timber and roofed in rusting iron that had never smelt paint. Bullnosed verandah packed with old bedsteads, cupboards, square kerosene tins, enamel basins, a wooden barrel fraying out like a wilting flower, a rocking chair.

The cottage was long empty when Lukey came upon it. Lukey moved in, disturbed nothing but rats and possums from the stove until the little flue sent up a pale blue thread against the dark of the cliffs.

***

Lukey had a gift for women – his eyes offered a mirror in which they might see their womanliness – reflections they may no longer catch in their husbands' gaze.

Rumours trailed Lukey like smoke that could not be ignored.

Not that any women knowingly shared their knowledge.

But still, talk of Lukey somehow escaped – stories grew until men spoke of it – wonderingly – not of course that it affected them – but how did the little bastard do it?

He wasn't big, or good looking, or rich – he didn't drive a car, seldom played cricket on the village oval, though when he did he had a wicked leg spin. Nor did he ride in rodeos or drink in Mick Dooley's –

And yet – women smiled at him, spoke his name with a small lilt to their voices like they knew some special thing about him.

***

'That little Romany bastard been around here then has he?'

'Who d'ya mean Dan?'

'That little gypsy Lukey Pease. I seen them quails in the safe – he's the only one round here fools with things like that. Bless ya money, tell ya fortune, steal ya blind – take whatever ain't screwed down he will – and more besides.'

'Oh Dan, don't be silly – he's a nice little feller Lukey – cut some kindling for me, gave me them quails, showed me how to cook them – thought ya might like them for ya supper.'

Dan spat.

'Eat em ya self if ya got a mind to – I'll have a proper meal chops and potaters and all the rest – can't do a day's work on crap like them quails.'

Dan sat hunched over his mug of tea, dipping thick biscuits into it.

'I hear stories about that Lukey. He's a gypsy see? – ya can tell by them eyes and that dark skin – that's the Romany in him.

'They got ways with animals and that, like them quails.

'He ain't got no gun, how's he get them quails? Them people runs with the carny people – not too fussy to hire their women out neither – carry knives they do the lot of them, women too, use em too soon as blink. Got their ways them Romanys have.'

'How come you know all that stuff? Women and knives and like that?'

Dan shrugged, reddened. 'Ya take care who ya let in the back door.'

Mavis laughed. 'Oh Dan – there's no harm in Lukey.'

'I hear what I hear – You pay me mind now.' Dan rose from the table. 'Think I'll go down to the pub.'

Mavis watched him go. How could he know all that stuff about Lukey? Lukey who could have his hands under her dress in a moment natural as breathing no right or wrong about it with Lukey. Easy as eating.

And things was different afterwards – for a sweet while afterwards things settled in their proper place, the breeze blowing through the leaves carried fresh scents, the calls of birds clearer, sweeter – the grass softer, the sun warmer.

Whereas Dan – well, Dan did keep a roof over their heads, no doubt about that, something that did not figure at all with Lukey. But Dan – well – Dan might leave her feeling like she wasn't that much ahead of the slop bucket – jamming her against the wall afterwards, snoring – she would just lie there and listen to him and eventually his snores would deaden her down into thick sleep.

But nobody warned about Dan.

They only warned about Lukey – like he was something dangerous.

Dan suspected alright – he just didn't know what he suspected – never do for him to find out.

But Lukey – well – Mavis was not about to give up Lukey.

Her skin felt silky and alive where Lukey had touched. She ran her fingertips over places where Lukey's had been – remembering small pleasures they had left in their wake.

She took down a hogget hindquarter from the meatsafe,

sliced through four loin chops then split them off with the cleaver. She curled the fatty tails around the bone and put them in the baking dish, three tablespoons of dripping fat with a bit of the brown jelly from the bottom of the dripping bowl, pumpkin, potatoes, flour and salt and onions – put the dish in the hot oven.

She shelled peas put them on to boil, added salt.

Mavis looked at the little plum-coloured quails in their striped coats of bacon, rude white apple sticking out between their legs, put them on a tin plate, popped them in the oven beside the chops.

Twenty minutes and they filled the kitchen with their heavy scents – no sign of Dan, she took the quails out and ate them, dark and sweet and juicy, bones like matchsticks – hint of apple and rosemary – he knew a thing or two alright, Lukey.

***

Lukey might sign up for a job of fencing and maybe for a month or six weeks he would turn up at the appointed hour and do whatever was required. If he was building a set of yards the rails were smooth, knots and lumps adzed to silk. When he morticed rails into posts, set the butt end in the socket, there would not be room for a cigarette paper in the spaces between. When he strained a wire fence the wire sung.

Lukey had a store of jokes he dealt like cards in a poker game, and he played poker like he was telling jokes – but he seldom lost at cards – not even if they were just playing for matches, which they were most of the time. Mostly the men gave their money to their wives. The wives might give them back a bit of beer money, gone by half way through the month – another two weeks before the eagle shat.

Lukey always had some money about him. Money and a little knife – a slim blade that slid out of the bone handle at the press of a button – Lukey cleaned his nails with it at smoko.

Lukey might carve a hollow stick into a whistle in minutes, little holes along it, play a tune before smoko was over, toss it to the kid that made the fire.

Lukey was the last person a man might notice in a group.

But a woman might feel the warmth of those dark eyes, catch excitement from the flash of teeth in a face of glove leather, be careful not to show it.

A woman might hide a secret smile, run through bits of things that maybe needed fixing, recipes for fancy cakes and biscuits sitting long years unused in the kitchen drawer.

Remember stories.

Yet it was Alma – the glow of a young bride about her, wide smile and laughing eyes, young body open in its grace, her Robert off with the fettlers for the next month – it was Alma laughed at something he said, touched his arm in her easy way, tossed her head and pointed up the hill to her house.

It was Alma's butter churn that Lukey made the new arm for, fitted it onto the old spindle, carved a knob that spun so she could turn the handle and never change her grip.

It was Alma who sat beside him, watched his clever brown fingers shape the wood, squeezed him a glass of juice with oranges fresh from the tree in the yard, smelt the cinnamon smell of him, watched how the dark curls clung behind his ear until she must reach out one finger and catch one, uncurl it and let it go like sprung silk, while Lukey worked on the handle.

It was Alma's fingers played with the dark curls, the skin on the back of his neck soft as the inside of her satin slip, played over that brown skin and Lukey turned to her – teeth so white and eyes so full of possibilities they choked a quick little laugh from her.

***

Lukey built Alma a little dressing table for her bedroom, built it out of old cedar, dovetailed and pegged and glued, not a screw or nail anywhere in it – a little drawer in the centre and a framed mirror on pivots behind, polished with many coats of shellac and spirits until it glowed with a richness that fingers ached to touch.

He brought it up to Alma's house on the back of the sulky behind old Tom, brought it up in pieces wrapped in an old blanket and pulled up by the back gate, carried it piece by piece through the sunny morning while Alma watched silent on the verandah, back of her hand to her mouth.

Lukey set it on the verandah, set the top on the carved legs, fixed the frame of the mirror in its little holes in the top, whispered the drawer into place, closed it and when he looked up Robert was standing beside Alma.

***

Lukey's face darkened, brown eyes muddied, his lips a tight slit.

He stood head down – put the adze aside when it glanced off a knot of wood and grazed his leg, slicing a cut in his grey pants.

'Some cunt's been digging fuckin holes with this – blade's blunt, chipped see? – bounced off the stay, like to cut me fuckin foot.'

'Any you bastards been digging holes with Shagger's adze?' Big Jim Cullen, ginger haired overseer of the crew building the yards. Jim looked around – all heads down, carefully busy.

'Nope, don't look like no one here Luke boy,' grinning. 'Must of bounced against them crowbars in back of the dray.'

Lukey looked at Jim Cullen unsmiling. He'd tied the razor edge of the adze in its fold of old leather like he always did. The big red bastard would have taken it out himself, dug a hole to shit in – Lukey had seen him do it before. Loose the edge on an adze and it'd bounce off the ironbark, take your leg if you weren't quick.

Lukey was quick.

But that dressing table.

Taken him three weeks to build that dressing table – match the grain in the legs, carve them out, steam the curve on the table front, sand it all smooth, boil the glue down in the old brown pot, cut and fit the dovetails, drill the peg holes, taper the pegs, fit it all together time and again until it sat tight and neat as one of them Chinese puzzles, peg it and glue it, let it set.

And then another two weeks for the polishing. Rub and shellac and rub again, eight coats, more in places, till it had a deep red glow to it and every eye of grain in the rich wood opened and looked back behind thick eyelashes – took a lot of work to get that finish, bring out the heart of the cedar.

Maybe his best piece – but no more than a match for Alma – fresh open generous, with the dew still on her and needing a man bad after her husband had woke the sap in her and went off with the fettlers gang.

And now the dressing table lay smashed in the road outside

her gate, shards of mirror flashing careless fire in the morning sun. Something twisted deep and bitter in Lukey but he didn't check his stride, didn't glance at the cottage, didn't see the blotched face by the kitchen window.

Robert hadn't hit her. He'd just looked at the dressing table and his face had shut down and he'd went inside – took his hat and walked out the door, shut the gate, headed off down the road to Dooley's without a word.

He'd come back late that night, still didn't hit her, but hurt her bad and deep – worse than if he'd hit her – used what had been between them to hurt her in ways she had not thought possible – left her bone cold – bleeding in places that should never bleed.

In the morning he'd went back with the fettlers gang – she'd heard the snapping and crunching – discordant music of shattering glass by the gate and what little warmth remained had drained from her.

Later she'd stood by the window and watched Lukey walk past and she'd felt something tear inside, seeping down her legs.

***

The yards were part of the new railway siding. Heavy ironbark rails big as sleepers side-cut into ironbark uprights foot and half thick – four rails to a panel, each rail heavy as two men.

Lukey began on the bottom rail, cut the mortices into the posts, trimmed the rail with the newly sharpened adze, rested the rail in the side-slot of the post, worked on the one above, and then the one above that.

Big Jim Cullen bored the bolt holes – bulging muscles twisting the hand brace through the unyielding ironbark –

curled corings falling with the bittersweet resin of freshcut wood.

Jim started at the bottom rail.

The bit was through the rail and deep into the post when the top rail fell, brought the next rail with it, landed on Jim's arm holding the brace, snapped the steel bit deep in the post.

Jim screamed when his new elbow speared white and red through freshly smiling skin – it took two men to lift the rails off his arm, freckles vivid against suddenly pallid skin, sweat darkening his ginger hair.

***

Lukey found Alma sitting in a red smear by the sink, teeth chattering. He carried her to the tub, boiled a kettle, bathed her in warm water and crushed ti tree leaves, soothed her torn flesh with ti tree oil, fed her brandy and honey and warm water, lay her on the bed, covered her with the down quilt and stood looking at her pale shivering, stripped and laid himself under the quilt beside her, held her cold body against him until the trembling stilled and she slept.

Alma's cottage caught fire that night, burnt to the ground as timber cottages will – nothing but grey crinkles of corrugated iron in the ashes, black block of stove, tilting sink and a brick chimney. No trace of Alma.

When the fettlers returned a funeral was held in the small wooden church – Robert scattered a jar of ashes in the churchyard.

'No – I ain't going to put up no stone for her. Not wasting good money on no stone – still owe a hundred and fifty pound on that there heap of ash back up the creek. Take more'n a year to pay that off.'

Robert spat in the ash at his feet.

***

'He's got her in that shack back in them cliffs. I seen a black snake mesmerize a frog once – frog couldn't move – snake swallered it whole. That's what them gypsies do with women.'

Jim Cullen – right arm in a cast dark with sweat hanging from a sling around his neck, a glass of beer clamped in the fingers of that cast – raised the glass to his lips with the outward swing and bobbing head of some badly designed piece of machinery.

Sweat ran from his red face like water from a full sponge.

'How ya know?' asked Robert.

'Seen her meself – went shootin rabbits, come on this little shack real quiet, up there back of nowhere – seen your Alma plain as day hanging out the washing and here's this little gypsy in the rocking chair on the verandah, big speckled dog an all.'

Jim Cullen took another neck stretching swallow from his glass, wiped the sweat from his face.

'How d'ya know it was Alma? How could you tell from so far off?'

'Mate – them tits, that arse – no offence mate – yeller hair flashin – ya couldn't mistake that woman for no one else hereabouts.'

Robert downed his beer, ordered another.

Jim Cullen peered at him. 'What ya going to do about it then?'

Robert shook his head, stayed silent.

'Can't leave her there mate – can't leave her there with that dirty little gypsy bastard – ain't right mate – ain't right what them gypsies do to women – ya can't leave her there mate.'

Robert said nothing, drained half his beer.

'We'll help ya mate – we'll help ya, won't we boys?'

***

Jazz took Jim Cullen in a silent rush, leapt at his throat before Jim knew he was there. At the last moment Jim raised his plastered arm and the dog's teeth closed on it, knocked them both to the ground, rifle clattering on the rocks.

The dog released the cast, worried his face – snarling – tore an ear.

Men scattered in the dark. .

'Hey you bastards come back – get this fucken dog off me.'

Jazz vanished.

Jim Cullen staggered to his feet.

Running feet faded into the night.

Jim lumbered after them, cursing.

He passed within five paces of Lukey, standing by a tree a rock in his hand, Jazz silent at his feet.

Cullen was ten paces past him when Lukey threw the rock – it tore the air with its sigh, hit Jim Cullen with the sound of an axe biting timber. Cullen fell.

Lukey stood motionless, hefting another rock, watched the

dark bundle that was Cullen slowly separate itself from the ground, groaning.

Shapes came back, lifted him between them, bore him feet dragging into the night.

Lukey returned to the dark gleam where Cullen had first fallen, picked up the rifle, fingers traced the deadly shape of the little butt-loading Browning, the big buckhorn rear sight – tossed it down the old well.

A slow light bloomed in the cottage, Alma silhouetted in the doorway, hair silk in the light. Jazz padded up the steps, laid his muzzle by her legs, tail rapping the doorjamb.

Alma could see Lukey's teeth before she could see him.

He grinned at her, shook his head, tossed the rock into the night, brushed his hands on his trousers.

'You okay?'

Lukey nodded. 'They'll be back.'

***

Morning sunlight crept down the cliffs, stirring white cockatoos into screeching flight.

No smoke rose from the little flue in the rusty roof.

No dog lay carelessly by the verandah steps, no horse grazed quietly in the meadow below the cottage.

No sulky stood shafts down in the grass.

THE ENGLISH TEACHER

Raz Gartner's got this Playboy Black Label on his desk and he and Jim McGuire are looking at it. You can't see across the oval for the rain.

Pete Anderson is doing a cartoon of old Rumbleguts on the blackboard. Rumbleguts is Mr Snelling, the Headmaster. He's always farting, silently, doesn't think anyone notices but you can tell another one's on the way by the noises his belly makes. Borborygmus – I looked it up – that's what Rumbleguts's noises are called.

The door opens and in walks this woman, dark hair and olive skin, – daggy old grey coat about as sexy as the tarp on the cricket pitch – she just walks over to the desk and stands there, Pete's wiping the blackboard as quick as he can.

Everyone quiets down.

'Hello everyone, my name is Jane Ackermann, I'm your English teacher.'

She takes her raincoat off – there's a daggy grey dress under it – she shakes the coat and hangs it behind the door and gives her head a bit of a toss and all this dark hair swirls about for a moment then she picks up the roll.

'I'll just call through the roll and ask each of you to stand up in turn when I call your name.'

Raz Gartner's got a horn when he stands up and there's a bit of a snicker. Raz is sixteen, the oldest in our class, serious pimples, but Miss Ackermann just calls out James Hall.

Raz grins around and sits down.

Raz calls me Einstein, but it's got a sharp edge on it.

I won the Maths prize last year, and the Latin and Ancient Greek prizes too I guess.

Raz is halfback for the First Fifteen – it's unusual to have someone only sixteen in the Firsts. When he's not calling me Einstein he calls me tapeworm –   long and thin. Sports elude me.

Miss Ackermann calls out James Meredith and I stand up and say 'here Miss Ackermann' and she gives me a little smile and her eyes are really warm – and I suddenly see she's actually quite pretty. When she smiles there's this faint dark line above her top lip.

I smile back and I sit down.

We do some poets that day – I remember we do this Ozymandias by Shelley which Miss Ackermann attaches a fair bit of significance to – I guess it's a nice enough poem – I suppose he's talking about Egypt or something – it's not a bad English period, goes pretty quickly actually.

***

James Meredith stands up and says 'here Miss Ackerman' and gives me that sweet smile. Those gentle eyes and all that hair tumbling down his forehead, he has a poet's face – I mean it's a sensitive, responsive face.

My heart melts towards him, although I try not to let things like that show. But he always has some remark that delights me – that day he said

'Look on my works, ye mighty, and despair – it really means

the opposite of what he intended, doesn't it Miss Ackermann? What Ozymandias intended I mean.'

And that's the whole point of the poem and it was so sweet the way he said it, and little John Budden nodded.

Raz Gartner made a slurping sound.

He's the boy with the pimples and the erection.

***

I begin to really look forward to Miss Ackermann's classes.

Sometimes my mind wanders a bit and I do sketches – of Miss Ackermann mostly– I guess she thinks I'm taking notes.

I like drawing people – which Mr Lipton, he's the Art teacher, says is quite unusual.

My sketchbook fills up with Miss Ackermann, I get quite good at doing her. I think she wears that daggy dress to hide beneath, because sometimes when it presses against her there's some real shape under there – as time goes on she seems prettier, and her body more shapely – well, I keep imagining more shape.

Anyway, one day I draw her without any clothes on at all – except for the red vinyl shoes she wears – they've got high heels that shape her legs – she's got nice legs, small ankles and muscular calves. She looks great in this drawing – I've given her great boobs, the whole deal, she's reaching up to the blackboard.

I'm just touching up her nipples and the class is pretty quiet and I look up and she's standing over me looking down at my drawing.

I can't breathe.

She doesn't say anything and walks around behind me.

She leans down and shuts my sketchbook and picks it up and points to a line in The Ballad of East and West and says 'read the next verse please James.'

She says 'meet me here after school today James' and she walks back to her desk.

Raz Gartner says 'What's the matter Einstein, she take your colouring book?'

I stumble through this bit about a mare playing with the snaffle-bars, whatever they might be, and I have never felt so awkward in my entire fifteen years. I'll be sixteen on December 13, so it's more like fifteen and two thirds.

***

James Meredith's drawings of me are *very* unsettling – a bit flattering actually, but his sense of line and movement are excellent. I'm trembling when I pick up his book – I just don't know how to handle this.

I'm sitting at my desk when James opens the door after school and he turns bright red and almost steps back, but he stays in the doorway until I say come in James, and shut the door please.

I have his sketchbook open at the nude picture of me, the book is full of pictures of me, he's trying not to look – he glances down and reddens even more which I didn't think possible, his eyes look like he might cry.

I feel so sorry for him, I touch his hand and I say 'do you have sisters James?'

He nods.

I say 'do you look at them like this?'

He nods and then he says 'not when they know.'

I can't help smiling, I say 'you seem to know a lot about women' and he relaxes just a tiny bit and says 'not really – it's mostly guessing and photos, you know?'

He blushes again, his eyes are bright with unshed tears.

I tear the nude drawing out of his book.

 I say 'I'm going to have to keep this James.'

He looks so crushed – I can see he thinks I'm going to take it to the headmaster.

'I'm not going to show anyone James, it's just that the classroom is not the place for this sort of thing, don't you agree?'

He nods and a tear shakes loose from those beautiful eyes and trickles down that cheek that scarcely knows a razor.

I say 'you'll have to promise not to do this in class any more James.'

He nods and another precious tear breaks loose. I feel like a murderer.

I touch his hand again, from nowhere I say 'would you like to draw me outside of class James?'

He looks at me with those wounded eyes, he thinks I'm teasing him so I just squeeze his hand a little and smile at him.

 His lower lip is open but his mouth is not moving.

I pat his hand and I say 'well think about it James.'

God alone knows why I said that – I've just looked in through the gaping gates of Hell and they're starting to swing safely shut and I kick them open again.

He says nothing for quite a long time.

Then – 'yes, Miss Ackermann – yes please.'

My heart sinks and soars in the same moment because we are heading for dangerous ground here – but I can't stop now – the only hope was that he'd refuse, and I've talked him out of that.

He has art on Thursday afternoons – I hear myself saying 'will Thursday afternoon be alright James?'

And he tries to speak, his throat moves, but he just nods.

I say 'good! –'

I can hear this artificial breeziness in my voice.

I say 'we can catch the 315 bus after school, it's only twenty minutes to my place, will we meet at the bus stop at a quarter to four then?'

James nods again and he says 'okay' in a small voice.

Then he says 'thank you Miss Ackermann,' and I get up and he opens the door for me.

And I ask myself what on earth have I done?

And I know perfectly well, and I also know there is no power on earth, or above, or below, that can stop it now.

***

The English Teacher

I am naked under my grey tent dress all Thursday, I am literally quivering as I walk down to the bus stop on Thursday afternoon. There he is with his case and his art folder and something hot and juicy bursts inside me.

'Hello Miss Ackermann' he smiles down at me. I touch his hand and there's a small snap as a spark jumps across and I say 'lovely, James,' he smiles again and inside I am just a mess.

We sit in one of those double seats on the bus, I am painfully aware of him beside me as we fuss with our things – his art folder's on his lap and my briefcase is on the floor, I pick it up and we lurch against each other around corners and I just know that his awareness is as tight and explosive as mine – I can see this vein in my wrist beating like a butterfly with the pounding of my heart – when I glance at him I see a vein pulsing in that soft spot below his ear – my mouth is so dry I can't swallow and I get my water bottle from my briefcase and have a drink and it's better and I see him looking and I hold it out to him and he blushes, but he takes it and he drinks without wiping the neck God bless his heart and he hands it back to me and our fingers touch and another spark snaps – I can hear it and it stings and I snatch my hand away and we look at each other and we laugh.

***

The bus stops right outside her house, it's one of those houses they call semi-detached – like a house with a wall down the middle making two houses.

There's this little red-tiled porch and a few bushes behind the front fence and she opens this black door with a brass knocker on it and there's a hall right through the house with sunshine pouring through the glass at the far end.

Miss Ackermann walks down the hall to the kitchen where

the sunlight is and puts her bag on the counter. She turns to me.

'My flatmate's gone to see her parents in Perth, her mother's not well. Would you like some coffee?'

'Yes please,' I say, and I look around this big room while Miss Ackermann fills the coffee machine and says 'do you like cappuccino?' And I say 'yes please Miss Ackermann.'

Miss Ackermann finally hands me a mug of coffee and we sip for a while.

It's warm in here.

'Well then,' Miss Ackermann says – 'shall we begin?' And she reaches up and undoes the buttons of her dress looking straight at me and I'm watching her hands move down her front and she just sort of opens her dress and these gorgeous breasts fall out.

Jesus – there they are – so beautiful – full and dark-topped and wobbly –

I didn't expect them to be so *real*.

And she slides her dress down and it catches on her hips for just a moment and her navel is soft and deep and her belly is quite round below and it curves into this dark thicket of hair and it's so private I look back at her face – my eyes sort of bump over her breasts on the way, and she's smiling at me – I mean she's really smiling and she puts her hands on her hips and sways slowly and she is deliberately drawing my gaze to the centerline that runs down through her navel to that exotic forest and she raises her arms and I can almost hear a grass skirt rustling to the sweet movement of her body.

I can't believe people are *allowed* to do that – it's so bold –

so glorious.

'Well James, will I do?' She says.

My throat is so thick I can hardly breathe. And I say 'Oh yes, Miss Ackermann. You're beautiful.'

There's just so much of her – so much *shape*.

Mum asked the other day 'would you like a Walkman for your birthday James?' and Jesus would I ever. She's always giving me stuff, I think because she's not there much.

But now – well – I mean – Miss Ackermann naked is all I want for the next ten thousand birthdays.

***

I can feel James's eyes on me like hot hands.

It looks like there's a light inside, they're so bright, so eager.

I wriggle up onto the table, I lean back and I say 'would you like me like this James?'

I can see he would, but he's so tangled in emotions that his throat just moves and he picks up his art folder.

I say 'wait a minute James' – and he stops – 'if the model is naked I think it's only fair that the artist should be naked too – don't you think so James?'

He blushes, but he wants to be naked and he nods. I say 'well take your clothes off then James.'

I watch his dear face, he's so confused and excited and of course he takes off his shoes and socks first, then his tie and his grey shirt – I can count every rib on that sweet hairless chest – there's a mole beside his left nipple.

He turns away to undo his pants and I say 'James, look at me.'

So he undoes his belt and unzips his trousers and slides them down his long legs and his white underpants are poking out and he's standing there helpless and I say 'the underpants too James' and he pulls them down and it looks a bit painful and he straightens up

And Oh God

I can't help myself.

***

It's dark outside when I wake up.

We're in Miss Ackermann's bed, she's asleep beside me. There are pictures of dolphins on the wall and there is a big teddy on the floor, and two dolls. Miss Ackermann is lying there with the sheet caught around her feet, but the rest of her is not wearing anything.

For a long time I just lie and look at her.

Before we went to sleep she said 'won't you be expected at home?'

But Mum's not at home very much, and Justine and Sandra are both at Uni.

And Dad – well, Dad's got his music – and he doesn't really notice who's around.

So no – I'm not expected home by anyone in particular.

I get my art folder and I start to draw Miss Ackermann.

My pencil finds a life of its own – it flows over the page

caressing every curve and hollow of her –

She fills my head with her beauty and my hand needs no help from me –

I catch a crook of knee, a soft fullness of breast, a curve and cleft of buttocks, a dimple of navel.

She turns in her sleep and I capture every glorious line of her, the flow of her hair, the curve of her spine, the two dimples at its base, the glide of her thigh, the sudden tufted thicket, the separate beauty of her toes, the arch of her foot, the starlike fineness of her fingers, the small half moons on her fingernails.

Page after page I fill – and the thing is, when you're drawing well – really well – you don't need anyone to tell you because you know beyond all doubt that you are putting down your truth. And her beauty is my truth.

***

They hold Prize-giving in the School Hall near the end of term.

Raz Gartner gets the Ainsworth trophy for football.

I get the Maths, Latin, Ancient Greek and English prizes.

I'm really surprised – Miss Ackermann hasn't said anything, and it's not as if she hasn't had the chance.

She's wearing a white dress that really gets her shape, with a red belt and the red shoes – she looks great – Mr Beckham, the Gym instructor is fussing around her, pulling out her chair, getting her a glass of water like he's never seen her before.

I even saw Raz Gartner check her out when he went up for his prize.

Then Mr Lipton stands up to announce the art prize.

He waffles on about the high level of competition and the maturity of the winning entry –

And then he calls out my name.

Jesus!

I handed in a drawing of Miss Ackermann ages ago.

I drew it when she was asleep that first time, she's lying on her back with her head turned away so you can't tell who it is –

Well I could tell it was Miss Ackermann even if I just saw her foot, but I showed her this one and she said why not put it in the art prize if I want to, so I did.

I'd forgotten all about it.

I look up at Miss Ackermann and she's smiling at me. I'm really embarrassed, but I smile back.

The entries hang along the back of the dais.

The prize is this big book on Leonardo da Vinci, but I wish I hadn't put the drawing in.

Mr Lipton says the drawing holds nuances of tranquility and satiety and it's very accomplished. He keeps talking and shaking my hand. I wish he'd stop.

I'm glad Miss Ackermann can't hear him.

Mum's down in the front row. She hasn't seen the drawing.

Big deal. Mum cracks this big fake smile, Dad just sits there.

Afterwards Miss Ackermann comes up and says

'congratulations James,' and I say fairly quietly 'you didn't tell me about English,' and she smiles that smile that lights my world. She looks really young.

They bring out cakes and tea and everybody stands around talking and people wander over to have a look at the entries in the art prize.

A few people are hanging around my drawing.

Out of the corner of my eye I see Raz Gartner walk up there with Jim McGuire and he just stops – and then he leans forward and I watch him nudge McGuire.

I go cold.

McGuire gets this funny look on his face and he looks at my drawing and then he looks over at Miss Ackermann.

She catches the look.

Gartner looks at me and he's got this sly grin.

Gartner and McGuire walk over to me and Gartner says 'that's Ackermann – isn't it Einstein.' He's not asking a question.

'You've been sticking it to Ackermann, haven't you Einstein.

'Got yourself a bit of Jew quim there Albert alright – hot gash they tell me – kept a lotta krauts warm long winter nights at Auschwitz.'

I can't speak.

There's a roaring in my ears, but it doesn't drown out Gartner's voice.

Over his shoulder I can see Miss Ackermann watching us – going pale.

'That's how you got the English prize too – isn't it Einstein? Porking the English teacher. Greasy jew slut.'

Gartner and McGuire turn and look at Miss Ackermann, and she looks away, clutching her bag.

They walk back to the drawing, Gartner talking to McGuire. They look again.

Gartner walks back to me with the smile of a hungry dog.

'You tricky bastard – Einstein.'

And for the first time, there is something approaching admiration in his voice.

I look back to Miss Ackermann – she is hurrying down the Hall.

My feet have lost the power to move.

'There's laws about that sort of thing Einstein – paedophilia and shit like that.

'She'll do time, Einstein – think of that did you?'

***

Mum and Dad get a letter.

Mum waves it under my nose. Her hand's shaking.

The letter's cut out from newspaper print.

JAnE ACKeRmANN is FuCkING jAmEs MeReDitH

My art folder is open on Mum's desk.

'I love her Mum,' I say, and she slaps me really hard, grunting.

And she's screaming 'HOW COULD YOU JAMES, HOW COULD YOU DO THIS TO ME!'

And I say 'and she loves me Mum.'

And Mum goes really cold and says 'you're a child, James, a precious, gifted child, and she is a monster and she will go to jail.'

And I say 'no Mum, she's lovely and I love her' but Mum has shut her face down and she calls up Mr Snelling and demands to see him tonight.

We meet in his house because Security won't let us in to the school.

His letter is the same as Mum's.

Mum says 'Snelling how could you let this happen?'

And Mr Snelling says 'with all due respect Doctor Meredith we can't be sure anything has happened' and Mum says 'Don't waste my time Snelling –' and bangs my art folder down on the table and these drawings of Miss Ackermann fly everywhere.

'You will dismiss her of course, Snelling, and you will notify the police beforehand.

'Any decision of mine regarding the matter of you and your negligence will depend upon your handling of this.'

And old Rumbleguts sounds like a lorry starting up and he says 'yes Doctor Meredith' and a ripe green stink fills the room.

***

I leave home the day I turn sixteen.

They don't let me see Miss Ackermann before the trial. I get in to the courthouse because I'm sixteen now and anyway I'm not wearing a school suit.

Miss Ackermann looks small and pale – her eyes are dark, bruised – they scurry over the faces in the courtroom and then they find me and a small light flowers in them, spills into her face and heads turn to follow her gaze and I see her catch the movement and lower her eyes and the room grows cold.

She has no chance.

My drawings are displayed on large cards, passed to all the jurors.

My hand destroys us both.

Miss Ackermann is remanded for sentencing. Two large policewomen with tight hair and thick hips escort her from the glass-sided box to the top of those secret stairs.

She raises her eyes to mine.

Like mine, they bleed from mortal blows.

The night is dark with small rain outside the courthouse.

Traffic hurtles in headlong haste for the warmth of homes in an alien world.

I step into its roaring torrent.

FISH BEETLE

That's the first I knew they could bite.

When they brought that kid into me with these things buried in the flesh of his fingers, blood pouring from his hand, the kid was white, from shock as much as loss of blood, and he was only just starting to feel the pain. That surprised me, they could do so much damage without him feeling anything.

In the end I couldn't save two of the fingers, too much tissue had gone.

But maybe I'd better start at the beginning

Adamant – I love this little town, not least because of Cherry of the cheeky arse. I've always considered myself a tit man – but one glimpse of Cherry's jaunty bum in those ragged little shorts and I was lost. Not that she's shortchanged elsewhere, but that's what got me – and that smile, and the 'I'm game if you are' look in her eyes – green – green as the shoaling sea along the golden beach of Adamant.

It's a tiny place – the nearest town of any size is Eden – you've got to turn east off the highway and drive through twenty K of national park to find us. It's just a little road and someone keeps taking down the fingerboard at the turnoff.

So we're very private here – two hundred souls in winter – 'course there's a hell of a lot more in summer. I was Surgical Registrar at Westmead – second year in the slot – heading upwards at speed and well, what happened I won't go into now, except to say you can't cover up things like that and get away with it – not in my book – so I just quit, left them to it.

And I drifted, me and my motorbike and Joss – he's a little Shitzu that I couldn't leave behind, and anyway he likes it on the bike – and we wound up here in Adamant. Been here for a year now, and I'll probably stay forever.

A lot depends on Cherry of course – she's got itchy feet I fear, although that's sure as hell not all that's itchy. She's a trained nurse, even if her nurse's uniform doesn't quite meet your expectations – when she's wearing it that is. That's another thing I like about her. That and the fact that she can't resist Joss – who has decided he sleeps on the bed with us. God knows what he thinks.

So anyway, it seems little Dave Anderson and a couple of his mates are fishing for yellowtail off the jetty Saturday morning. The water's glass-green right to the bottom, not a ripple on the surface and the yellowtail are going mad. Dave and his mates keep them live in a bucket, sell them to the co-op for live bait. The kids love that, and it keeps them in pocket money, although I suspect Dave's share goes into milk and cornflakes. I mean I've treated Dave's old man, and Bob Anderson is not what you'd call a dedicated milk and cornflakes sort of a bloke.

More a rum and water type. Easy on the water.

Well, the yellowtail are going crazy this Saturday morning – the kids are using sugar-pickled prawns for bait – it's the best in my opinion, and in the opinion of the yellowtail. They've got a bucketful the size of a garbage can, and Dave's trailing his prawny hand in the bucket feeling the fish nibble his fingers while he watches the fish below swim around his hook.

One takes the bait and darts off and Dave brings out his other hand and there's blood everywhere – he doesn't notice it at the time, he's watching the fish on his line, but he's having trouble holding the line and that's when he looks down and sees them.

Anyone who's ever caught yellowtail for bait and seen those big blue beetles crawl out of their mouths – well, they're disgusting aren't they? – and so *unexpected.*

Yes well, when Dave looks down at his hand it's covered with these bloody blue fish beetles and they're digging into his flesh and the blood is making the line slippery.

Dave lets out a yell and shakes his hand and a lot of them fly off, but five or six have worked their way in there and when he shakes his hand again bits of finger fly off as well – by the time he gets to me two of his fingers are finished and the little buggers are in there chewing their way up. One's got as far as his wrist, and there's a lot of blood.

I manage to retrieve four of them with forceps and drop them in a Petri dish of ethyl alcohol, but the one at his wrist breaks in half and the head keeps burrowing and I have to cut it out – no time for a local and Dave yells when the blade sinks in, but he can't feel the head of the beetle at all.

I look at these things in the Petri dish and they look like every yellowtail fish beetle I've ever seen – maybe a little bit bigger, and of course they've gone purple with the blood. I incise one down the ventral median and mount it under the binocular.

The jaws surprise me – big chitin pincers, two on each side, one behind the other, and there seems to be some sort of gland in behind the front pair feeding into a groove in the hard black shell of the jaw – maybe they secrete a painkiller or something.

On the back of the thorax there's two little buds, just where the thorax meets the abdomen, something pricks in my memory but entomology was never my long suit.

Cherry calls the ambulance and little Dave goes up to Wollongong for micro-surgery to the remains of his hand. Cherry goes with him – I knew she would – I hate her to be out of my sight for even half an hour, but I don't say anything – little Davy needs someone, and it sure isn't likely to be Bob. Not unless you threw in a couple of free bottles.

Cherry knows – 'Get over it Pete, I've gotta go with the poor kid' – she gives me a kiss to go on with and I watch her climb her outrageous body into the back of the ambulance and I watch until the ambulance vanishes into the green of the National Park.

I wrote up my notes – I sent them to the A.M.A., but I didn't do anything more about the episode – or the fish beetles. Foolishly as it turned out. I was much more concerned about Cherry and what was going to happen to that gorgeous arse, and I got distracted – not for the first time of course. And anyway, who wants busloads of nosy departmental types clumping around here, turning Adamant into a three-ring media circus?

So a year later when Frank Adamson turned up with his hand missing all the way down to his wrist and scarlet everything and Dick Mitchell told me what had happened I wasn't exactly surprised. I guess in the back of my mind I'd known all along that something wasn't right.

What nobody ever tells you is what the navy does with its munitions waste.

Tom Davis – he's a fisherman down here now – he did time in the navy out of Jervis Bay. It's Friday night in The Adamant Arms, Frank Adamson walks in, toes poking from his sneakers and that sour slit of a mouth on which a smile never looks at home, and he buys himself a beer like he always does before he looks around the bar. He doesn't buy too many stray beers does Frank. Tom's telling this story and Frank sidles up and jabs an elbow in his ribs and says 'tell us what you know, it won't take long.'

I can feel Cherry fizz up beside me – she was listening to Tom – 'the only time that old shit smiles is at his own jokes' – but Tom goes on like nothing happened.

'We had to roll these canisters overboard out beyond the continental shelf – except that a storm blew up and we didn't quite make it out to the shelf.

'The word was they were depth-charges that had passed their use-by date, not primed of course, just old and maybe a little unstable. They'd been repainted, everything in the navy that stands still long enough gets repainted – grey as it happens – but you could see that divided circle of three wedges under the paint.'

'So what?' says Frank.

'That's the symbol for radioactive stuff – Frank' says Cherry, and I can hear the acid in her voice. 'Thought you'd know that – Frank.'

I'm surprised Frank doesn't drop dead from laser poisoning.

'Course I know that – what's the point?'

Cherry doesn't bother to answer. 'I need another brandy Pete' she says.

I wonder how Dick Mitchell puts up with Frank day after day on his boat. And I think of Lucas Heights. Now I'm not saying there's any connection – the fish beetles and those canisters – but still, I wonder.

Frank's passion was killing fish – the bigger the better – and that's what he spent his money on – all day out chasing fish with Dick Mitchell.

They'd come in with sharks trailing from the stern, or yellowfin hanging from the trawl arm, couple of times they even brought in marlin – sold them all to the co-op.

This day they get into a school of fish that look for all the world like giant yellowtail, Frank's using a new glitter rig, one of those pink jelly plastic things – Dick said they just drift through the school of them motor off, Frank casting with a slow retrieve – two hits – loses one, boats the other, hundred kilos Dick reckons.

When they get in to the jetty they winch it up and Frank wants a photo – Bill the co-op manager is there and he takes the picture – Dick's clasping the fish behind Frank who's got his arm up in the gills like he's holding it up. I saw the photo later – the fish is as tall as Frank, looks like a giant yellowtail. First real grin I've seen on Frank.

Then there's blood running out under the gills and Frank's yelling 'hang on you useless bastard' at Dick and the fish falls to the decking and Frank's hand isn't there – just a bloody stump spraying scarlet.

Dick says a great big fish beetle crawls out the mouth of the fish and Dick kicks it over the side. Dick winds heavy line around the wrist and it slows the bleeding – and for the first time in his life Frank is silent, looking at the hand that isn't there.

And then the pain hits and Frank starts screaming, and he's still screaming when they get him to me. I jab him with morphine and that slows him down – he's lost a lot of blood – his beard is mostly scarlet, and his shirt, it's run down his legs into his shoes. The only thing that's pale is his face, and that's usually the reddest part of him. I give him plasma and call the ambulance and they take him to Eden emergency, but he's D.O.A.. Shock'll do it at his age, even without the blood loss.

Next morning I go down to the jetty, Joss likes to come too early mornings. The sea has that glassy calm you get only for the first hour of the day – the water a limpid green, you can see every shell, every piece of weed on the bottom – little fish swimming around the piles of the jetty.

I'm not looking for anything in particular, and then I see it.

Rolling on its back, legs up, rocking in the slow wash of the tide. Dick's kick would have been a good one knowing Dick. And I just happen to have brought along my long-handled net with me, and a bucket. You know I hardly realized I had them? Let alone recall collecting them – but anyway they're going to be handy now.

I ease the net down into the water by the dead beetle – it's big, longer than my foot – and I just run the rim under the curve of its back and it slides easily into the net and I lift it up and onto the jetty and tip it out onto the decking. I reckon it must weigh three or four kilos. Joss goes berserk – barking his little head off, which is not like him.

As a rule Shitzus are not yappers, although he'll bark at a fox or something unknown in the dark – or at me when I'm late with his dinner.

Anyway, the way he's barking at this thing you'd think it was the most dangerous thing he'd ever seen – if he didn't have so much hair I'd say it was bristling, but the way it is you can't tell – but what he's blowing his brains over right now is a very big, very dead fish beetle. There's even a bit of a smell to it, like bad oysters. But it's just lying there, shiny grey-blue shell and all those little legs. I can't see its mouth.

I prod it with the net, but it's lifeless.

I nudge it into the bucket with the net and then for some reason I go down the landing steps and fill the bucket with water.

I'm halfway along the jetty when Joss goes absolutely mad and I look down and this fucking thing has its jaws wide open reaching for my fingers on the handle. Oh shit!

I drop the bucket and it spills this thing onto the wharf and it rolls itself into a ball like a giant fucking slater and I give it an almighty kick and it squeals this high-pitched squeal that goes right into my head and it bounces along the jetty and falls into the water and it's still squealing when it hits, and my ears ring with painful echoes as it sinks.

And these things come for it.

At first I think they're fish, but it's more beetles, there must be a dozen of them, they just arrow in on my ex-football and they form a cluster around it and the cluster drifts across the bottom out towards the mouth of the bay until it's out of sight.

I am not sorry to see it go.

Joss looks up at me and gives one yap, and I pat his snub little head.

That night is another one of those nights that make me wonder what on earth I managed to find of interest in my life before I met Cherry.

The sun is high over the ocean when we climb out of bed. I make coffee for us both and we stroll down to the jetty and Cherry spreads her arms wider than her smile.

'Oh Pete – can't you just feel that sun coating your bones

in happiness?'

And I nod, because that's exactly what I would have said if I'd thought of it.

Dick's down there, he's bending over something, and Cherry takes my arm and says 'Pete! What's that?' And then I see them.

On the wharf are half a dozen big beetles – just clinging to the edge, doing nothing.

I run down to the jetty, I grab an oar from the rack by the dinghies and I whack it down on the first beetle. It squashes in yellow ooze and I push it off the edge. The next one I don't get such a good hit – I almost think it dodges the oar, and it squeals that awful squeal that goes right through your head – Cherry and Dick are holding their ears and Joss is yapping his head off.

It's quivering this thing, and I hit it again and it falls in the sea and I look around for the next one, and you know? They've all gone. I reckon they got the message.

I look down into the water and I can see this beetle cluster just like yesterday's moving out of the bay. There's something about them that curdles my blood, makes me shudder.

'Jesus Pete, those things are disgusting! What the fuck are they?'

'I don't know – but the way they pissed off then, maybe that's the end of them.'

Which just goes to show how stupid you can be when you really try.

That night Joss whimpers a time or two – it's not like him,

he'll sleep through almost anything, and it's not as if we're being all that disruptive – he actually tries to burrow under the bedclothes and Cherry gets the giggles. It's not a particularly appropriate time to share with a dog, even one as small and fluffy as Joss – at least that's my view of the situation, and I discourage him, but I can see that Cherry's in two minds about it.

Next morning we stroll down to the jetty with our coffee – and oh shit.

The jetty is encrusted with big beetles all along its edges, side by side, there must be hundreds of them.

I grab an oar, but there's something different about them – they're paler, translucent – the sun seems to shine right through them, and they're not moving. Joss barks a time or two, but his heart's not in it. Dick's there too, he's got an oar now, and he walks up to the first of them and then it dawns on me.

I pry one from its clasp on the weathered timber of the wharf.

They're just shells, like the locust shells you find on trees, each one longer than my forearm. These things are all empty, split down the back, you can see the wing cases – of course! Those little buds at the junction of the thorax and abdomen were embryonic wing cases – and the head part holds the shape of chitinous jaws.

I'm glad I wasn't here to see those obscene giant cockroaches or whatever they were crawl out of their beetle skins and unfurl their insect wings, spread them till they hardened and then raise themselves on new-found legs and fly off. Joss must have heard them in the night.

The thought of *one* of those things landing on me, let alone a swarm…

Cherry looks at the crust of empty shells along the wharf, and then at me.

'Where have they gone, Pete?'

COCONUTS

Mary couldn't tear her eyes away from the hairs in Gerald's nostrils. It wasn't that she wanted to look at them, it was more that they had assumed a significance – an awful significance – heralding whatever might be coming next.

Something was coming – His adam's apple was bobbing up and down beneath a fringe of stubble his razor had neglected. In the pit of her stomach she just knew – She and Gerald had spent accidental time together these last ten days, mainly because Gerald was the only one remotely within conversational age in the resort.

Outside the car improbably slender coconut palms blushed in the sunset, mountains of volcanic plugs black jagged teeth along the horizon.

'Look at the sunset, isn't it beautiful?' she said brightly. Oh shit, might as well have said isn't it romantic – she was only trying to postpone the dreaded moment, but old Gerald was right into the beautiful sunset thing, his arm a patient python sneaking along the back of the seat.

She was only in the car because of Horace – Horace who spent his time sidling around the garden, dirty shorts hanging from a leather belt under a once-white singlet that might have looked better on a pig. A fringe of ratty hair over his ears slid down the back of his neck, dragging a large expanse of scalp with it. Sometimes he carried a rake or a sprayer, but mostly he seemed to be ogling her in a way that made her bikini feel much too small.

She had certainly never seen Horace actually do anything, like pick up the rotting fruit or fill in the ankle-twisting burrows with which unknown creatures mined the lawns. He didn't even collect the fallen coconuts, some of them embedded deep in the lawns from the velocity of their descent. Mary was a bit wary of the coconut palms.

Horace had been scrabbling around outside her bure – interfering with the plants immediately beneath her windows – and she hadn't wanted to close the shutters – that would be an admission of something – so when Gerald showed up and said 'like to go for a drive?' she'd jumped at the offer.

And now this. Not exactly out of the frying pan into the fire – more like into the warming drawer she supposed.

It wasn't as if she'd encouraged Gerald, all she'd done was not avoid him – how anyone could possibly take that for encouragement ? – and she'd only not avoided him because of Horace. She didn't find him attractive, not in the least, it was just that solitude led to Horace, and Gerald had been an easy alternative to Horace – well up until now he had.

Gerald was so *eager*, and he had a habit of snorting after he'd made a remark as if he wanted to withdraw it that Mary found irritating. *And* he wore those ridiculously small bathers which Mary determinedly refused to look at, although as far as she could tell from not looking there was nothing much to worry about.

She hadn't intended to be here on her own, but poor Louise had fallen and done something awful to her leg right at the last minute trying to get her suitcase down the stairs, and so now there was a spare bed in her bure. The last person she wanted to see in it was Gerald. Well no, the last person was Horace – Gerald would be second last. But out of the corner of her eye she saw the python had slithered to within striking distance.

'Oh God! I've been bitten!' she cried, leaping from the car, brushing frantically at her skirt. She raised her skirt, brushing at her thigh in search of the phantom insect, a search which of its very nature proved increasingly difficult, inadvertently revealing more than she intended.

'If it's one of those fire-ants they say you should lick it,' said Gerald. She could imagine Gerald's eager tongue already salivating.

'He didn't really get me properly,' she said quickly, lowering her skirt. 'Gosh is that the time? – I told Susan I'd be back at six for a massage.'

Oh God – Why did everything she said lead to hidden trapdoors? Massage clearly was not a good word.

Mary climbed back into the car and pulled the door shut wearing her best and brightest let's go now look. The python grudgingly retracted from the back of the seat, descended to the gearshift and they backed out into the little rutted road that ran past their resort to nowhere in particular.

***

The sun baked down on her back as she lay on the lounge beside the pool. The pool was apparently out of bounds to Horace, but Gerald would probably appear soon enough. Meanwhile the sun was so delicious that Mary just let it soak into her flesh, warming her into a careless torpor. She untied the straps of her bikini and lay face down, surrendering herself to the sun.

***

She woke to a cold breeze. The sun had vanished behind

thickening clouds that had purple bulges to them and a chill breeze rattled the palm fronds. Wind gusted abruptly out of the breeze, switching the tops of the coconut palms against the sullen sky. It had become suddenly dark. Mary gathered her book and towel and headed off towards her bure at the far end of the garden.

It was quite an isolated bure, and right at this moment Mary didn't like this particular part of the garden now it was dark, the small lights that lit the path not yet turned on and things other than the wind rustling in the bushes. The wind had become strong now, the crowns of the coconut palms thrashing the clouds, and there on the path before her was Horace.

'Oh' said Mary, and Horace grinned wetly.

She waited for him to move aside, but he remained right there, blocking the path.

She looked over her shoulder, but of course there was nothing there. She would have really welcomed Gerald now. A hand closed on her wrist and she turned back into Horace's bristled grin parting over stained teeth. His breath rose into her face, sour rum mixed with the memory of something dead.

She snatched her wrist, but he hung on.

'Don't touch me! Let me go!'

But Horace was surprisingly strong. She tried to pry his fingers loose with her other hand but he simply grabbed her other wrist and grinned.

'Let me go!' she shouted, and Horace let her go – and hit her – hard – in her stomach, and all the air went out of her lungs. She tried to breathe but her lungs would not suck air.

A grinning Horace took one unresisting arm and dragged

her into an open patch shielded from the path by bush. Mary was striving to regain her breath but her lungs still would not obey her. Horace pawed her and she slapped him, but it was a feeble slap at best.

But Horace slapped her back, and Horace meant business. She felt her teeth cut into her cheek beneath that slap. Her head ringing, Horace spun her, twisted her arms behind her and bound them with something. It turned out to be his belt, a fact she wished she hadn't discovered when he turned her around to face him. She gathered a shaky breath and tried to kick him in the pale patch where his shorts had been – not that she wanted to but what else could she do?

For a moment it looked like Horace might trip over his shorts, and her bare foot definitely made contact with something, although she half wished it hadn't. Horace grunted and the grin slipped from his face, and with her first really good lungful of air she shouted:

'HELP!'

Horace hit her again – he hit her stomach in exactly the same spot and this time she thought she might actually die. Agony burst open in her belly and it just took all the life out of her. Black ice filled her head, her lungs could not even begin to think of drawing a breath and she sagged to her knees. Horace pushed her backwards and she fell flat, her head bouncing on the grass.

Horace lowered himself on her and she lacked even the strength to roll away – she could see the coconut palms flailing above her – she felt Horace's hands pawing her – she had an image of those heavy leather gloves she'd seen on construction workers – she felt him jabbing at her – she braced herself for some scalding invasion and Horace flung himself against her with an odd sound, a mindless grunt, a lunge so savage it drove any vestige of hope from her trembling lungs.

***

Drenching rain revived her – warm dark torrents flooded her face.

Horace lay on her like a crocodile whose gaping jaws had at the last moment failed to close.

Gradually she gathered her strength until she was able to slide his inert body to one side and she could slither out from under him.

She climbed shakily to her feet and looked down at him.

There was something wrong with the back of his head.

She bent closer.

What had been bare scalp was now a flattened reddish mess.

Nearby, washed clean by the rain, glistened a large coconut.

MICE

I never liked mice – dirty crawly little things – run up your skirt before you know it – but right from the start there was something different about these 'uns.

Well the colour for a start– if you could call it a colour. More like glass really their fur was, like a fur of glass you could see right through to their nasty pink skins. At first glance they looked white.

Then their eyes. Purple they were, purple as a poison bottle, and they kept cocking their evil little heads from side to side like they was trying to get a better look at me. Them little eyes sent shivers up me I'll tell you, almost wet meself I did, first time they settled on me.

They moved different too – just the three of them, touching each other all the time with their little raw noses.

I didn't like them one little bit.

'Scat!' I shouted at them and they scuttered away through that dark hole down in the corner behind the dresser. I set the bin against it to make sure they didn't come back.

Cat was never around when she was needed – out after baby birds like as not. I heard them wagtails setting up a chippery snappery little fuss in the grape a while back – pound to a penny it was Cat after them. I caught her looking up at their little nest in the vine couple of weeks back – she's a smart one Cat, knows when they're growed enough to make it worthwhile climbing up that grapevine – not easy for Cat the size she is now – but she's partial to baby birds.

She was a good mouser in her young days – play with a mouse for hours she would – let it go, run a little bit – put a paw on it, just a little needle of claw sinking in to make sure it didn't get away – then let it go again.

Sometimes she'd just hold it with a paw on its tail.

She might bat it about a bit when it started to slow down – then crunch.

Sometimes she'd eat it – and sometimes she'd drop it in my lap. She knew I didn't like that, but it never stopped her.

Anyway, she isn't here now, and those mice – I'll set some traps tonight.

***

Well! All that noise in the night – silly old Cat got herself caught in a trap and did she yowl and carry on! Must have put her nose in it. Then she got another on a paw and she clattered around the kitchen screeching and yodelling knocking all me plants off the windersill – tipped over the bowl of milk I'd set for the cream to rise – she must of come in the winder 'cause I never let her in when I'm setting milk.

I had to get up in the dark of night and couldn't find the matches for a bit and when I did light the candle – what a mess it was. I threw Cat out the door and shut the winder and went back to bed, but I couldn't sleep. Not a wink.

And in the morning them mice was back in the kitchen, dirty little feet tracking milk all over everything.

When I saw them I picked up the big carving knife and just then they all bunched up and come jibbering across the floor directly at me – right through all the milk.

Well – I swung the knife at them, all bunched up like that and I missed them, but the edge sliced down through them pink tails and they come off and twitched around in the milk like scaly pink worms.

And how them mice did squeal! They looked that funny with their tails cut off, all three of them, blood spurting red curls as they squittered around in the milk trying to bite themselves where their tails had been.

Lordy I laughed.

Never seen such a sight in me life.

ALL MEN

'All men are paedophiles at heart' said Janet.

We sat in the outdoor bar of the Raddison hotel, Nadi, Fiji, killing time for our plane back to Sydney.

I was looking at this girl – body bursting with promise, careless extravagance of hair – moving with the dewy grace of youth – shorts of frayed denim just meeting at her crotch – smooth of skin dimpled by her navel reaching up under a top that flapped – no sag, just bouncing jut.

I don't know how long Janet had been watching me watching her – but I tore my eyes from those honeyed limbs and turned to Janet with her sardonic face, lines of bitterness bracketing her mouth. She didn't smile when she looked at me – as if what she said was an eternal truth that held no trace of humour – as if she were reading lines etched clear on the bottom of my soul.

And of course she was.

And it was that recognition that ignited a slow hot fuse deep in some part of me that lived a quite separate life to my civilised brain – separate to my public posture of philosophy and reason.

For my uncivilised self was already making plans for this girl who chose that moment to look up and see my soul with a knowledge she could not have had time to acquire – a knowledge she could only have been born with – and she smiled at me as if all things were possible and not many of them offensive.

She had the full lips that paler women strive for with botox – full lips that parted easily over big white teeth – and a red hibiscus in dark sun-tipped hair and there was nothing in her but the ebb and flow of nature's currents.

Janet made some sort of grunt and rose noisily from her chair – 'Don't be disgusting Roger – I'm going to have a shower, and so should you. A cold one.' And she flounced away.

Well it was as much of a flounce as one could expect from flesh whose sap had largely withered.

I turned back to the girl on the grass below and thought there were many things worse that paedophilia – and she looked up at me as if she could read what passed for my mind and she raised one hand behind her head and flipped her hair and her hips took on a sweet sway as she walked to the edge of the small balcony and she said – 'Hullo Honey – you want girl?"

And I looked into those soft brown eyes full of amusement and knowledge and I nodded 'Yes' and it came out dry and thick and a soft hand reached under the rail and rested on my knee.

'You got a room here Honey?'

I nodded again.

'You want to take me there Honey?' and the small hand slid up under my shorts – just a little way – but it was loaded with purpose and it seared my skin.

'We go Honey? – We go your room?' And I nodded and rose awkwardly from my chair and it occurred to me that Janet and all of the others might be watching – and none of that mattered worth a damn.

She stooped under the rail and crawled through and she

wore no bra and she followed my glance and took her time and her smile ripened and there was excitement in her eyes – she was still young enough to be stirred by the prospect of money and a room in a good hotel.

I wondered if reception would let her pass and the woman looked at me and the girl and I smiled and the woman smiled down at my ten dollars and we walked down the cool polished hallway to my room.

She walked before me, bouncing with the spring of the very young, flashing white teeth towards me to make sure I was still following – she reached back a hand to take mine and wrapped my arm against her side, against the warm jiggle of her flesh and she reached up and whispered in my ear

'I love you darling' and she giggled, and I found myself giggling with her.

I pushed the card into its slot in the door and for once it worked as it was supposed to – the green light flashed and the handle turned and we were in the air-conditioned elegance of the vast room with its indecently huge bed and she gazed around and clapped her hands and leapt up on the bed.

She bounced a few tentative bounces and then she slid off her shorts and stood straddle legged on the bed and pulled her top over her head and if you have ever seen a dusky orchid unfold the lush velvet of its petals in the evening light you might guess a small part of how she looked as she offered such a treasure.

The telephone drove shrill fingers into that room and I refused to answer it.

But its shrillness would not abate – it pealed and screeched with an urgency that refused denial.

And like a fool I picked it up.

'Roger! Thank God – quick – our plane is leaving early – the bus is outside waiting for us now, we're all in it, it's leaving in exactly two minutes.'

And I looked at the red flower in those dark curls, I looked at the sweet treacle of those limbs and knew I would not meet their like again – and for a moment the plane seemed far away – pointless – and then I picked up my packed and waiting bag and smiled at her and shrugged and gave her fifty dollars for the sweetness of her promise – she kissed me for that – and I left.

They were sitting deep in wicker chairs around the bar, *Mai Tais* in their hands. Janet led the raucous laughter.

LIBERATION

The troop-carrier grinds to a halt in a swirl of dust and sand. Around us collapsed mud-bricks mark the boundaries of the town square of Bazghat. Incongruous doorways and windows clutch at tattered masonry. Vultures, Allah's Chickens, perch here and there on elevated rubble.

In the centre of the square a dark crumple marks what might have been a fountain – or in this waterless place more likely a statue. Twisted shells of cars cluster blackly on metal rims and the orange hammer of the sun beats down making a cookpot of the metal troop carrier. I had thought the childhood back lanes of Booligal, trapped on the edge of shimmering saltbush plains, were hot. But midsummer noon in Booligal is early morning in Bazghat.

'Private Strong, see those little kiddies over there?'

The voice is Sergeant Frank Williams – red headed Sergeant Frank Williams, decisive, and with an unexpected singing voice that might charm angels from their perches.

I look across the square at two small shapes huddled in the shadow of a tangled car.

'Yes sarge.'

'Get those poor godforsaken kiddies, Private First Class Jason Strong, be a good fellow and get them back here on the double, and let us get our Christian arses out of this shithole.'

'Yes Sarge!' I say, and step out of the metal door, hot to the touch, leaving my rifle behind.

And the sun beats down. And the smell. The sweet stench fills my nostrils, my throat – I force my suddenly unwelcome breakfast back into its uneasy place and stride briskly across the square.

There is a dark rustle in the carcass of a car as I pass. Allah's Chickens hop and flap reluctantly from its depths, heads and necks glistening with juices not to be contemplated.

The two shrouded shapes look up as I approach – small brown faces with dark eyes large as children's eyes are large, but old and wise as children's eyes are not. The twisted car that shades them has bloated shapes in bulging fabrics that my eyes choose not to define.

I hold out the purple sparkle of Violet Crumble Bars, red cans of still-cold Coke, and their hands reach.

Their small fingers touch the cold cans and for a tiny moment a child-like joy flickers in those large dark eyes before the weight of too much knowledge dulls them again.

And in that moment my heart tears open for them, for they know the random rain of death as cruise bombs commit their mechanical suicides.

They have watched that rain fall all around them, and somehow they have survived – survived into a world where survival is no prize.

I take their hands, they grasp their small school-bags stuffed with whatever pathetic remnants children might scavenge in such a place – one perhaps a girl, the other a boy – it is not easy to tell.

A sudden whump behind me and I turn to billows of black smoke as Sergeant Williams ignites the interior of the car where Allah's Chickens fed. He has a jerrycan of diesel and old oil and a little petrol for such occasions – the petrol for ease of ignition, the oil and diesel for a longer-lasting burn.

As I lead the children from their small shade Sergeant Williams sloshes his mixture over the bloated shapes in the car beside them. The children turn to watch, the little girl holds out a hand, says something that might have been Ma! and might just as easily not, and Sergeant Williams flicks a match into the interior and the flare hits us like a hot pillow as the flames swell – for a moment we all stand mesmerized.

A small popping, a hissing sizzle, a muffled sigh as gas-filled cavities vent their perfume into the already over-scented air. I tug the hands of the children until they turn from this irreverent funeral pyre and we move back to the troop carrier, soldiers shuffling sideways, making room.

Hesitant white teeth flicker in small brown faces as barley-sugars, biscuits, nuts appear – the children stuff the offerings into their schoolbags, and I wonder if in this war without shape or boundary or definition of any sort, it might not be these children that will be the one small harvest of hope.

There are smiles, there are 'what's your name, darling's?', but there is no conversation on our bumpy roar back to Base Camp, no reply from small mouths and silent eyes.

We wind our way in through the sandbagged maze to the only gateway in the impregnable perimeter of Base Camp. We stop. Salutes are exchanged, documents examined, heads are counted, the red and white barrier rises and we roll beneath it into the safety of Base Camp.

Sergeant Williams guides us to the Command Post – an open tent of many desks where seated officers chase elusive columns of supplies or map the phantom movements of phantom enemies.

I stand beside the troop-carrier as Sergeant Williams leads the two small children, clutching their schoolbags like passports to a now-dead world. Eager hope precedes them, smiling eyes follow them – a female Captain stands with outstretched arms, the Commanding Officer rises from behind his desk as they wend their way towards him.

The children stop, turn to each other, reach into their schoolbags, and in that instant I know we are about to graduate from a school where the children have become the teachers.

The bulk of the troop-carrier saves my life.

The blast knocks me to the ground, one side of my face a gristled stub of ear, eyelid no longer able to close over seared eyeball, but the side of the vehicle shields me from the swift scythe of metal and body parts.

I am awarded a medal for my part in the Liberation of Bazghat – on the steps of that far memorial where truth has long died, where politicians' follies have become glorious battles for liberty and democracy, a green place free of Allah's Chickens.

I don't use mirrors any more, but for the ceremony there has been judicious use of bandages.

The bleak eyes of Beatrice Williams capture me. 'He loved children you know. We planned for our own ...'

Even in their posthumous generosity, there are no medals for the compassion of her sergeant.

They assure me that plastic surgeons will restore me, but I doubt their scalpels will cut deep enough for that.

Liberation

SALT FLY

We'd been at University together Tom and I, swum on the same team, stuff like that, not best friends – until that College re-union a month ago we hadn't bumped into each other for ten years.

So I was surprised when he said 'Richard how'd you like to go fly fishing for Golden Trevally up behind Fraser Island? Sandy shallows – tailing Goldies hunting yabbies on the flats.' It sounded good after the grinding lead-up to Christmas – *Everyone* wants their stuff finished by Christmas – they've got to get away to Aspen in January, or maybe it's Sapporo this year.

Anyway, I jumped at it.

Tom asked did I mind if his wife and kids, Jonathon and Mary, came too, she didn't fish, and of course I said sure.

I hadn't married, never found the girl – or the courage maybe.

But Rachel was so much more than I had expected of a wife for Tom – Tom was a doer, pragmatic, not confused by life's uncertainties.

Tom made all the arrangements – Brad and his boat for five days, a suite of rooms overlooking the marina – air-conditioned – essential up there that time of year, but no room service – other than beer.

We ate dinner that first night at the Boat Club, an aquatic version of the RSL. Rachel and I ordered prawn cutlets –

sponges soaked in warm oil. Tom was talking to Brad and a couple of guides that had flown in to do a story for a fishing magazine – they talked of the Coral Sea, Bonefishing on Christmas Island. Money was never an issue with Tom – and these guys were eager to sell him his next adventure.

Jonathon was running around with a bottle of Coke, Mary was making baby noises in her stroller and Rachel just sat there rocking her. I saw her try one of the prawn cutlets and then she just stuck with chips and beer and watched Jonathon over her shoulder and smiled at Brad and the other guys. I wondered if life with Tom was turning out quite the way she had expected.

Tom was a big guy – pretty fit – grinning, pushing an argument, looking for the best deal, the hottest fishing spot – he worked in a merchant bank, worked hard at it – and he played the same way. The guides loved it, kept coming up with offers – Chile, Alaska, the Seychelles .

I smiled at Rachel across the table and she smiled back in an easy, open way that made me feel part of her world. She had a generous body – toned, active – and she moved easily in it. She flicked a prawn cutlet over the rail and a seagull caught it in mid-air.

'Hope it doesn't kill him,' and there was conspiracy in her smile.

Tom missed the flying prawn – he missed all of them – mine included. Not the seagulls though.

***

The marina five-thirty in the morning and Brad collected Tom and me, the water glass, sun just rising, a little open boat with carpeted deck, centre console, poling platform above the outboard.

We assembled our rods – Brad asked Tom how he liked the Innovator and the Waterworks reel – I could see he was impressed. 'Haven't seen one of those before' he said of my rod.

The motor rumbled us slowly out of the marina and then we snarled our way across the rippling glass to a far shore. Water paled above wide sandbanks. Brad carved broad feathered loops across the shallows – 'Looking for rays, dolphins, dugongs, the Goldies follow them sometimes.' And I watched our sweeping curves with renewed interest.

Sure enough dolphins broke the surface in water barely deep enough to hold them, but no tell-tale golden flashes. 'Keep your eye out for nervous water' said Brad.

Ten minutes and Tom pointed to a shimmering patch in the distance.

'Good spotting Tom.' Brad cut the motor and climbed onto the platform with his long pole. Tom flipped a coin for first cast and I found myself on the carpeted bow – Brad had tied a white *clouser* onto my leader, a thing of small white feathers and metal eyes meant to look like a small fish. We crept closer.

'Look at them tailing!' said Brad, silver tails hand-span wide waving in the air as the fish nosed yabbies out of the sand.

'Long cast – metre to one side of them – now!' called Brad.

I made my usual trout cast, but the rod was unexpectedly heavy and the clouser had a life of its own. It rapped the edge of the boat and then caught in the slack line and the cast collapsed on the water.

'Again! – Quick!' called Brad, anxiety in his voice. This time my fly landed half way towards the tailing fish – a muffled grunt from Tom.

'Retrieve – cast again!' called Brad and I made a long cast that fell right amongst the waving tails. They vanished.

'Strip!' yelled Brad, 'strip fast!' and I hauled my fly line in as dark shapes torpedoed towards our boat and speared away in swirls of mud and sand.

'Goldies' said Brad – first school I've seen here since Christmas.'

Tom shook his head.

'Your turn Tom,' I said, stepping down from the bow, and Tom quickly took my place.

***

We scoured the flats for two hours as the sun rose hot and hard – dark shapes of sting-rays drifted slowly – shovel nosed sharks half buried in the sand, brown-backed turtles poked their heads up into the morning, but we saw no more Goldies, and we left.

Out by The Pylon Brad cast a hookless popper on the ocean and dragged it bouncing back across the water. Swirls followed it – big fishy shapes. 'Queenies' said Brad – and Tom flicked a clouser effortlessly out into the swirls. Within seconds he had a strike and for twenty minutes he played flashing, diving silver until Brad could drag the big fish in by the tail.

'Great Queenie, Tom!' said Brad, shaking his hand, slapping his back.

'Well done Tom' I said, but missed the proffered hand then

made a late fumbling clasp.

'Beginner's luck' said Tom, but none of us believed it.

***

The sun grew so hot we could not stand barefoot on the carpeted deck. There was no shade save for our hats, glare beat up from the shards of sea and the boat hammered into hard small waves as we chased fish on the lumpy top of the ocean. Needles of sunlight pierced my head. My face scalded and still the sun beat down, still we chased fish, the land a purple smudge at the edge of the world.

Finally we turned for home, battering across the washboard sea, my tender brain jolting in the bony cage of my skull, spray coating my polaroids with salt. A long hour later we eased into the calm of the breakwaters cupping the marina.

'Leave your gear in the boat – I'll wash it down for tomorrow' said Brad. 'Same time in the morning?'

'You bet' said Tom. I cringed inwardly as I stepped out of the rocking boat onto a stationary pier that continued to rock beneath my feet.

I stood for ten minutes under the cold shower, the heat slowly leaving my face, the vice of searing sun and jarring boat gradually easing its clamp on my skull. The tiled shower floor rolled uneasily.

Tom poured beers for Rachel and me, Fourex Gold. Salt and vinegar chips. The sitting-room was blissfully cool, beyond the windows the sea looked benign.

'What a day we had, eh Ricky boy?! How about those tailing Goldies – man they had you in a dust – take it easier tomorrow – get your cast ready sooner.'

'Tom, I think I'll give it a miss tomorrow.'

'Dad! Can I come tomorrow instead of Richard? Can I? Please Dad?!'

'Hold on Jonathon – Richard, you mean that? You really want to give it a miss?'

'Dad! Please, take me! Take me!'

'Yeah Tom, you take Jonathon – he'll love it. I'm pretty well knackered.'

'What about the afternoon – would you feel more like it after lunch?'

It was the afternoon glare and the rising chop that had really finished me. 'No Tom. I'll give it a miss altogether thanks.'

'Well son – looks like you got yourself a ride in the boat.'

'Yeah Dad! – Cool man – cool!'

'Will he be alright Tom?' from Rachel. 'You'll bring him back if he gets seasick or tired, won't you?'

'Sure sweetheart, sure I will – but he won't get seasick – chip off the old block, aren't you Johnny boy, eh?' Tom ruffled Jonathon's hair. Jonathon wriggled like a puppy.

'You bet, Dad.'

***

We ate that night at a café by the marina – Tom had asked Brad to join us and the prospect of having the tailing Goldies to himself next day made him expansive. He ordered two bottles of wine and talked fish to Brad. Rachel sipped her wine and idly rocked the baby in the stroller – she wore a light blue dress that seemed to have a lot of buttons undone. As she rocked the stroller it gaped over softly mounded flesh untouched by sun. She looked across and caught me watching. She smiled at me, held my gaze, and I felt myself smiling back with my whole body.

I flicked a look at Tom – but he was deep in conversation with Brad. Jonathon hung over the railing watching a sea-eagle. He'd thrown a bread roll into the water and fish were butting it around and the sea-eagle swooped down and plucked out a fish neat as you like.

'Dad! Dad! The bird caught a fish! Dad! Look!'

Tom glanced up, but he missed the moment of drama. 'Sure son – '

***

I heard them leave at five o'clock. My bed rocked a little in the night, but it had settled now.

Later – and there was Rachel naked in the open door, sun behind her, holding glasses of tomato juice.

'Bloody Mary's Richard?'

She started to climb into the bed, a movement that stretched out for a longish time – my eyes were soaking her up, she seemed to be watching my eyes, but it was one of those sweet moments with no awkwardness, just a slowly building anticipation that pretty soon moved beyond our control.

Everything about Rachel was generous – and she wasn't one of those women who shave their body hair. I read somewhere that body hair captures pheromones, and something certainly worked its magic that morning.

***

Afterwards we both lay there feeling vastly pleased with ourselves.

'Is that what tailing fish do?' she asked .

'Not while I was watching.'

After a while Rachel said 'you know, that was the first time I've been unfaithful to Tom,' and I could think of nothing to say.

And then she said 'if we do it again, is that being unfaithful twice?' and I said 'I think it only counts as once,' and she said 'oh, good.'

***

'I was surprised when I met you,' I said.

'Oh?'

'You're not what I would have expected in Tom's wife.'

'What were you expecting, Richard?'

'I don't know, some sort of hockey jock, I guess,' and Rachel laughed.

'Dance – that's what I did. I loved ballet – but they said I was too tall.'

'Does Tom go to the ballet?' and Rachel laughed again.

'Tom goes to the Rugby Club.' And then she got this serious look.

'Tom's a good provider – and he's good with the kids when he's got time – those things are important.'

'Yeah – sure – '

She raised her arms over her head and gave that glorious body a huge stretch and collapsed back.

'You're thinking if he's so great why am I here with you?' and there was a vulnerability in her eyes.

'There's something about you Richard – I get the impression that you really like women. I'm surprised someone hasn't talked you into marriage before this.'

Well of course I like women, but there aren't too many like Rachel – well none that I can recall. I didn't know if I wanted to say that, so I stayed silent.

'You look like a little boy, and yet last night when you were practically slavering over my tits I knew it could be like this. These days as far as Tom's concerned I might as well be titless.'

'That's careless of him' I said.

'And besides, with two small children it's not as if the world's exactly full of opportunities for adultery – unless it's the air-conditioning repair man, or the meter reader, and they've never seemed quite my type, somehow.'

Rachel's feet were up my end of the bed and she rolled on her side and bent one knee – I knew it was deliberate even as I straddled her leg and slid up to the glistening centre of her and she twisted to look at me.

I wanted this to last for the rest of my life and I daren't move and yet whether I moved or not small liquidities were having their way and I hung in there way beyond where there was any point in hanging in and my thighs clamped hers and my greedy hands clutched her and our bodies heaved towards enlightenment or destruction – and we clung until there was nothing left and still we dared not draw apart, the junction of our limbs slick bristled curls.

***

It took some time to return from that far place, and I think we both knew that it was no ordinary country we had glimpsed.

'I don't' think I want to go on without you Rachel.'

And she snorted 'Jesus. Richard!

'It's so easy for men to say things like that – they don't have to make commitments to children, to family. Men just think "great fuck – let's have more."

'But what do I tell Johnny when he asks where's Daddy? Huh? Do I say Daddy got pissed off when I fucked Richard?'

'Hold on Rachel, hold on –' but she was beyond hearing.

'Never mind about Mary – she's too young to know – there'll just be space in her heart where Daddy used to be– she only learnt to say Daddy the other day. She'll be alright, won't she Richard?'

There were tears in her eyes now, but she couldn't stop.

'And I'll look at myself in the mirror and if I catch a shadow of Tom behind me – oh yes, Richard can't do without me I'll say – and if I see you smiling at your secretary I'll know it's just one of those gosh you're a good secretary smiles – of course I will, won't I Richard?'

And the tears fell.

'Can't we just –'

'We can't just anything Richard – anything we do will mean deceiving Tom – and I won't do that.'

'It's a bit late for that' I said. 'We haven't exactly invited him to the party.'

'I'm not deceiving him. There has been no opportunity to tell him – no chance to pretend this didn't happen.'

'That's splitting hairs Rachel – you and I are deceiving him by betraying his trust.'

'Oh God, Richard – his trust! Do you think Tom gives a thought to what we might be doing while he's out fishing? He just hopes I'm fawningly grateful for being brought up here to this Tropical Paradise.'

She grabbed the coloured brochure from the bedside table – flapped it on the bed. 'Have you seen how they promote this Other Eden? '

She riffled the pages. 'Every page, dead fish – men, women, children holding up dead fish. Gutted fish. Fish with their heads snapped back – dead fish and cans of beer. I should be swooning!

'And the only thought he gives you is you helped pay for the boat and the guide, and how he's got it all to himself. He calls that winning – may the best man win – and clearly he's the best man – the strongest stomach, the hardest head.'

Maybe – but perhaps Rachel found herself in a prison whose bars were the children that she loved. And us – we had both jumped over an easy cliff, and found the cliff much higher and the water far deeper than we had ever imagined.

'I'll tell Tom,' I said. 'I'll tell him tonight.'

***

Lions. When they take over another lion's pride, I've read they sometimes kill the young cubs.

I mean you need time for kids to grow on you. You need to see that belly swelling to vast size and then have your world completely inverted by the demands of a baby. That's how you get used to kids. Slowly the baby turns into something that a man can recognize as a human being – and that's how it happens.

Not by taking on someone else's ready made ones.

But Rachel did not come individually gift wrapped.

'You must buy the complete set sir – they are unique pieces sir – hand painted originals – matching, sir – no, we cannot break the set sir.'

And I wondered if I could afford the set.

***

'Dad nearly caught a whale! It almost ate us!'

Jonathon burst through the door wide-eyed and febrile, weariness etched in the tender skin of his face, Tom behind him, grinning. Rachel and I were sipping gin and tonics in the sitting-room, the sun on the golden rim of the world. Well I was sipping mine, Rachel was spooning custard into Mary's mouth.

'No John! No. I don't believe it.' Rachel wrapped him in her arms but Jonathon pushed himself back.

'He did Mum, he did! It nearly came into the boat! It was huge!'

Rachel looked up at Tom and he grinned and nodded, grabbing a beer. She turned back to Jonathon. 'Tell me about it, darling.'

This really big whale came up to the boat and Daddy hooked it but it got away.'

'Just as well by the sound of it, darling.'

'Yes, he got a sucker instead.'

Rachel looked at Tom.

'A remora from the whale took my fly, sucked on under our boat.'

'Tom! No! Was it dangerous?'

Tom shook his head. 'I think he knew we were there, just came up to have a look.

'But Ricky boy, talk about tailing Goldies! – you should have seen them this morning – five schools. You've never seen anything so glorious!'

Well, that depended on your perspective.

'I caught two – one would have gone thirty kilos Brad reckoned. What a day – eh, Johnny?!'

'It was cool Dad – it was just the greatest – can I come again tomorrow?'

'Richard's turn tomorrow,' and Tom looked at me.

A deep silence opened up between us then, a silence into which almost anything might have fallen.

I glanced at Rachel, but she was wiping custard from Mary's face.

And it was then I discovered that the great boulder of truth was a weight my courage did not own the strength to lift and toss into that void.

Slowly I shook my head. 'Got a touch of the sun yesterday, Tom. Give me another day back here, see how it goes.'

Jonathon's eyes lit up. 'Oh Dad! Yeah! – Can I come?

'Brad reckons tomorrow'll be calm but it could blow Wednesday – tomorrow could be your last chance Richard.'

I thought about that.

'Thanks Tom – I'll take my chance on Wednesday.'

Tom nodded, but there was eagerness behind that nod.

'Well my big strong young man, if you're going out again with Daddy, it's early bed for you tonight.'

'Ahh Mum – not yet' but his drooping eyelids betrayed him.

***

'He slept in Jonathon's room – didn't want to disturb me.'

There was a hint of loss in Rachel's voice that threatened to drain the life from the morning.

We reached for each other, but all we had was desperation overlain with guilt, and it left us empty.

'I'm not being truthful, am I?' she asked. I said nothing.

'I want to escape from Tom's world – I can see that now – but I don't want to hurt my children.'

She fell silent, swept her long hair back, baring a soft throat to the fates.

'But if I go on submitting to Tom's world – little by little it will erase whatever it is that makes me what I am – I'll become no more than his vision of me, and then he won't see me at all.'

And Rachel wept, her tears warm on my skin.

'For a while I thought you held one of the keys Richard –' and I looked at her. 'You need two keys to open the door to the magic kingdom.' She shook her head. 'Tom doesn't have one.'

'You do,' I said.

'Perhaps you do too Richard – maybe there are many doors, and our keys don't fit the same door. But still, you have opened something – and I can see now. Maybe you and I won't go on together, but I can't go back.'

And it occurred to me that having betrayed Tom, we then betrayed ourselves by our failure to tell him – and that second betrayal cost us our world. Perhaps Rachel's keys are ours for one bright chance, and if we fumble, if we prove inadequate, then they fall from our grasp and the door closes.

I began the small business of packing my bag for the noon plane south.

'Tell Tom my office called, I'll ring him,' I said, and Rachel nodded, but she was looking out at the Marina, and she didn't turn.

HIGH TIDE

Norfolk pines stood behind the seawall in the little park facing the inlet, a sheltered bay with a jetty jutting on the northern end. A playground beneath the pines held childrens' swings, a small turntable, plastic tunnels.

The playground was alive with young mothers and small children – the mothers surely not old enough to be married, let alone have children of their own. And although the air carried the shards of autumn the women seemed all to be wearing tops with scooped necklines, nipples erect, proclaiming their femininity, their fecundity, skin soft as peach fuzz, young and appealing and he'd better not stare, someone might notice.

He felt left out – these women deep in the jungle of breeding and nurturing their young, escaping for a moment from a world of sticky fingers, dirty nappies, demands for instant gratification to bright afternoon sunshine in this park lapped by pretend seas.

The Kikuyu turf ended in a seawall of sandstone blocks. Yachts jiggled at their moorings in the bay, pointing north like a school of obedient fish, the chime of steel halyards against aluminium masts making gentle elfin music.

A ferry surged in to the pier at the end of the jetty, screws at full reverse thrusting a bulging stern-wave – a metal hulled catamaran that tore the waters of Broken Bay, crossed the open heads at speeds unimagined in the days of the smoking chugging wedding-cake ferries of his youth.

Every square metre beyond the park contained new, multistoried statements of architectural significance – nature pruned and trimmed lest she impinge upon the glories of stainless steel and glass glaring orange in the lowering sunlight.

As he drew close to the sea wall he saw the tide was in – the strip of beach below the wall shrunken, the sand lapped by pretend wavelets, unchallenging to the straddle legged steps of the smallest toddler. Even now two small naked figures were waist deep in the gently shoaling waters.

High tide – the best fishing tide. Little fish followed the tide up the sands, bigger fish followed the little fish –

Little fish have bigger fish that bite 'em

Et da capo ad infinitem.

Ogden Nash? His mind didn't always supply cross references with its trivia.

The ban on commercial fishing had allowed fish stocks both large and small, to re-build in the bay.

He had caught bream, kingfish on the incoming tide. In spite of all the imposts of civilisation, the tides still ebbed and flowed twice every day. He'd read where super-wealthy residents further up the bay had built sea walls in front of their houses – built them at the low tide mark and then filled in behind them – claiming it was their land.

The law said land between high and low tide was public land, but the excessively wealthy residents – part time residents anyway – they'd said the tides had altered because of council dredgings or some such.

Lawyers fattened on the debate while the public walked across empty front lawns or were shouted at or even soaked by malicious lawn sprinklers. He thought the tides might one day claim the lawns in spite of whatever the lawyers were paid.

A particularly gorgeous blonde caught his eye down on the beach close to the wading toddlers, a scooped brown sweater that provided an invitation to at least pneumonia. Her companion wore a grey turtleneck, the fabric so thin her nipples all but pierced the gossamer weave.

He walked along the top of the wall – seagulls fluttered in the sea at the corner by the jetty. Normally they gathered around families eating fish and chips, but it was mid week and the fish shop was shut, so now the seagulls were doing what they did best – fishing.

Swirls ruffled the water – kingies chasing pilchards, the seagulls garnering the chopped fragments, the baitfish fleeing down the shallows towards him – choppers boiling the surface, seagulls fluttering up, dropping down, seething down the shoreline.

A silver kingfish burst out of the shallows – long as his arm it landed on the beach – flapped wetly silver back into the sea – god if only he had his fly rod, could cast a fly into that roiling mass.

He'd done that one time, around on the ocean beach – a school of salmon had trapped a great dark cloud of baitfish in the angle by the pool, the salmon darting shapes feeding in ankle deep water thick with tiny fish.

Three times he'd cast his fly, three times he'd taken salmon so big the tip of his rod bent around parallel to the butt until both pointed at the fish. A kid had been standing on the rocks with a landing net, scooping salmon out of the ocean. He'd only seen it that one other time close to the shore, although he'd seen gulls diving into frothing schools of baitfish well offshore while big fish chopped them up from below.

But just that one time close to the shore like this – and yet, not quite like this.

Here the water heaved in long powerful surges – big kingfish leaping high – something huge was chasing the kingfish – driving the school down the beach – opposite him now – there – a black shape long as a nightmare, swift as death – striking at kingfish right beside the naked toddlers – one child snatched sideways in a sudden swirl of red – then floating free, truncated, trailing a forest of crimson tendrils.

The swirlings vanished.

The seagulls furled their wings, floated, white ballet slippers sitting on a silent sea.

The blonde in the brown sweater began to scream.

CLARISSA

Clarissa wandered down the dusty road switching at dead thistles with a stick. Sometimes the thistles exploded in white clouds, sometimes they just snapped and fell into a rustle of dry prickles.

Clarissa had nothing else to do, nowhere else to go – she was fifteen and no one wanted anything to do with fifteen year old freckles or frizzy red hair that refused to obey a brush and shook off ribbons on Sunday mornings. Her mum and dad had gone to the Oxley's for lunch, and if there was one person Clarissa hated more than herself it was Jamie Oxley, followed closely by Mrs Oxley, who had a way of looking at her like her undies were dirty.

'Of course I'll be alright by myself Mum – don't worry. And besides I've got homework to be in Monday morning.'

She'd already done the homework and Mum had given her a bit of a look – but they'd gone anyway – dust rising behind the old grey Chev ute with its frost of dead grasshoppers on the radiator grille.

It was Dad really – and Mum knew it. Lately Dad had a way of jamming a hard lid down on her day and grinding it until all the life was squashed out.

'Don't lounge like that Clarissa – ladies keep their knees together.'

It hadn't always been like that – Dad had ridden her in front of his saddle out mustering for hours before she was old enough to go to school. Carried her on his shoulders holding her legs while she spread her arms and flew.

But not now.

Now it was 'do up those buttons Clarissa – ladies don't let their shirts flap open' – and Dad didn't seem to hear the 'oh Bill' from her mother.

Clarissa thought red headed people got hotter in summer than ordinary people – her armpits were slidy, her underpants were clutching at her and sweat was running out of her hair into her eyes. Even the stick was slippery in her hand. She took one last savage swipe at a thistle head dislodging a shower of thistledown and a large golden orb spider. She let the stick go, came to a standstill in the shade of an ironbark tree.

In the distance a plume of dust headed down the road towards her, a plume of dust with a flashing bead at its point, a bead that gradually grew into the windscreen of a car. Well a truck actually, in fact the old red Ford truck with the wooden wheels that was the Oxley's, the flat windscreen shimmering over the corrugations.

She could hear it now, the uneven rattle of cylinders that had no rhythm to it, as if the engine couldn't decide whether to stop or keep going – the erratic sound matching the random flicker of the windscreen. By the time Clarissa recognised the truck it was too late to hide, and besides the ironbark was the only tree along the road for miles. She'd look pretty silly if she suddenly ducked behind it.

She brushed at a sticky cluster of flies trying to drink the sweat from her eyes. Jamie Oxley – that's who was driving, she could see the fluff of his fair hair.

The truck rattled to a muttering stop beside her tree, the dust collapsing in a small shroud over them.

'Want a lift?'

The very last thing Clarissa wanted was to sit beside Jamie Oxley in his noisy old truck, but she nodded, opened the little door with its hot little handle, stepped up on the running board, climbed in and sat down – horsehair poking through the crazed black leather of the seat prickling the backs of her legs.

At least there would be fewer flies when they got moving, and in a choice between Jamie Oxley and the flies, Jamie won by a small margin.

'I thought you were coming to us for lunch' said Jamie.

'Is that why you're out in the truck, so you could dodge me?'

'What about you?'

'I've got homework.'

'Yeah sure – I bet you did it Friday.'

'How do you know that?'

Jamie shrugged.

It was nice bumping along the road without any flies, and the breeze cooled the sweat on her head, snuck up under her dress in a pleasant if slightly embarrassing way.

'What else d'you think you know about me?'

'You're younger than everyone else in our class – and you like poetry – and people think you're stuck up.'

'Who thinks I'm stuck up?'

'Well, most of the boys do, but I think they're a bit scared of you.'

'Scared of me? Why should they be scared of me? Do you think I'm stuck up?'

'You have a way of saying things makes them feel stupid.

'And no – I don't think you're stuck up – I just think you're a bit brainy.'

'Brainy? You're the brainy one Jamie – the essay prize – maths.'

'Until you came along –'

Stuck up. How could anyone call her that? Terrified is what she was – terrified of everyone looking so neat and smart and knowing, normal hair and ordinary skin – she was a freak, that was the truth of it.

'You've got green eyes –you know that?' said Jamie.

'Of course I know that – I can't bear to look in a mirror. Why can't I have blue eyes like you?'

The dark line of trees etching the creek into the wide brown plain wobbled towards them.

'Feel like a swim?'

'I haven't got any bathers' said Clarissa.

'Me neither – '

Clarissa looked at Jamie, head boy of their small school, smiling, golden skinned and her stomach gave a small lurch.

She nodded her head.

'It's very hot – ' and the places where the sweat had cooled on her turned to little hollows of ice.

Jamie drove the old Ford down the side track by the bridge, wound along beside scraggly redgums to a clump of Acacias and Coolabahs guarding a bend of the creek. Water glinted through the trunks.

Jamie switched off the truck engine and for a while there was no sound but the harsh cries of crows flapping awkwardly out of thick leaves, and when they had gone the cooling crinkles of the truck.

'Well – here we are then,' said Jamie.

I can't believe you actually said that thought Clarissa, but what she said was 'Yes.'

The seat was prickly against her legs, flies regrouped around her eyes, her mouth, her nostrils. She could not move, not even to brush away the flies.

Jamie too was congealed in his seat, as if the enormity of the next step was simply insurmountable.

The hot blanket of silence was pierced only by clicks and whirrs of brittle insects. A magpie chortled into the void

'It's too hot, let's get out' said Clarissa, and climbed out of the truck, scraped her way through the trees towards the water. Jamie followed.

A bright green line of thistles fringed the creek at the edge of the trees, grey water-smoothed creek-gravel shelving down to brown water that moved imperceptibly downstream like thin gravy. It had a cool muddy smell.

Clarissa stepped gingerly through the thistles, prickles spiking her legs, took off her shoes and socks and stood barefoot on the creek-gravel. The hot stones burnt the soles of her feet.

'Ouch – it's hot.' She slipped out of her dress, pranced carefully down into the creek in singlet and underpants. The water was cool, the bottom deepening to slimy mud under her toes. She ducked her head under and opened her eyes to a dull brown world and when she surfaced Jamie was walking into the creek in his underpants.

He was surprisingly skinny, she could have counted all his ribs, she wanted to tell him it was cool and lovely but she thought he might be embarrassed to know she was looking. He slid into the water, surfaced in a spray of brown droplets.

'That's nice' he said.

Clarissa bobbed under again and emerged shaking her hair, water flying in arcs.

'I like your hair' said Jamie.

'You couldn't be serious – it's yuk!'

'No – it's beautiful – it was just like a rainbow for a moment there.'

'I'll swap you any time.'

Clarissa watched Jamie climb out of the water onto the gravel, buttocks pink through wet underpants. She clambered up the bank herself.

'How are we going to dry things? – Jeez these rocks are hot!' said Jamie.

'I suppose we could take our undies off and spread them on the rocks – I mean I can see right through yours anyway – it can't make all that much difference' and Clarissa pulled off her singlet, stepped out of her underpants and spread them on the gravel. 'You shouldn't be looking.'

'I can't help it.'

'Well, if you're going to look you'll have to take yours off too.'

Jamie pulled his underpants down, spread them on the rocks, stood up.

Clarissa laughed, Jamie blushed, turned away.

'Sorry, I didn't mean to be rude. Does that always happen?'

'I haven't been naked with a girl before.'

'You can turn around you know – it's okay. Quite interesting actually.'

'You don't have freckles under your clothes.'

'I know.'

'And red hair…'

'Well what did you expect?'

Clarissa sat on her dress, looked at their undies drying in the sun.

'Know what I found in the back of Mum's desk?'

Jamie shook his head.

'Lady Chatterley's Lover – the book. I was looking for stamps.'

'Wow. You read it?'

'Yes – have you?"

'Bits of it.' Jamie blushed.

'Yes. Well it's a bit slow at first, all that coal mines and stuff – but I really liked Mellors and Connie – I read it all night.'

'It's banned you know.'

'Of course I know – but why?'

Jamie blushed again, looked down.

'What? You mean all those words – ?'

'I guess so' said Jamie.

'Kids use them every day at school – '

'Yeah – but not in books.'

'Why not? He's only trying to be honest in that book'

'How d'you mean?'

'He's only trying to show how sex turns to love – why ban that?'

'They say it's depraved' said Jamie

'Depraved! All he does is talk about Mellors putting his – well – in Connie's – you know. What could be more natural than that?'

'Would you like that?'

'No!' Clarissa laughed. 'Well, when I'm alone I imagine all sorts of things – I mean listen to the girls giggling at school – maybe you could call them depraved...

'But now – here – with you – in the flesh –' Clarissa giggled. 'I can't think of anything worse.'

'Well thanks' said Jamie.

'Oh Jamie – I didn't mean it like that.' Clarissa laughed again, touched his arm. The touching might have been a mistake. 'I just can't see how people ever get around to it.'

When she'd started to say it, it was true, but by the time she had finished it was already a lie

'Yeah – but they do.'

'I know.' And she did. That was the trouble – answers came before you were ready. She had to keep talking before something happened – she wasn't sure what, but if she didn't say more words it was going to happen. 'They do it. And then they ban books about it – and encourage wars – Why?'

'Wars are exciting I guess –' said Jamie. 'Specially if you're stuck out in the bush or something. Wars are like free travel when you can't afford it.'

'So it's okay to kill people – it's just not okay to write books about making love – is that it?'

'It does sound a bit weird when you say it like that' said Jamie.

Clarissa found words had deserted her. She didn't mind actually – for a moment her eyes caught and held Jamie's and the spiky fence of words she had built around herself seemed a pity – something she wished she hadn't done.

Was there a gate in that fence?

Would Jamie find it?

***

'Where have you been Clarissa? Your mother and I were that worried when we came home and there was no sign of you. And what were you doing in the Oxley's truck?'

'Jamie gave me a lift.'

'What do you mean – gave you a lift? Where were you?'

'I went for a walk down the road and Jamie came past in the truck and it was hot so he gave me a lift.'

'A lift to where?'

'Well, it was hot so we drove down to the creek and had a swim.'

'Did you have your bathers?'

'No – we swam in our undies.'

'You ought to have more sense – swimming in your undies with boys at your age. You're practically a woman.'

'Oh Dad! It's only Jamie Oxley.'

'Doesn't matter. That doesn't make it right.'

'Bill – that's enough. Clarissa's a sensible girl – I'm sure it's quite alright – Jamie's a nice boy.'

'He's a boy Sarah, he's a boy. And Clarissa is too old for that sort of thing – look at her – much too old.'

'Oh Dad!' and Clarissa left the room, banging the door.

'Now look what you've done' said Sarah.

'It's not what I've done – it's what those two have been up to.'

'Stop it. I don't want to hear any more of this rubbish – she's your daughter too for god's sake.'

'Mark my words – That's all I'm saying – just you mark

my words.'

***

Things were getting impossible lately – well ever since Mum had discovered Lady Chatterley in the drawer of Clarissa's bedside table.

'What were you snooping in my drawers for then?' said Clarissa.

'I wasn't snooping – I was just putting some of your clean clothes away.'

'Well, what's the matter? – it's your book anyway' – and Sarah had looked quite startled – and then smiled in a not quite guilty way.

'I'd forgotten all about it – where did you find it?'

'In the back of your desk – I was looking for stamps.'

'You might have asked me could you read it.'

'Oh Mum! As if –'

There was a pause as they both studied the thin red cover with its gold lettering.

'Does Dad know you've got a copy of Lady Chatterley's Lover?

'Of course he does', but Sarah blushed as she said that.

'Mum! He doesn't, does he.'

'Well, I can't actually remember if I told him or not.'

'Oh Mum.' And Clarissa giggled. 'Has he read it?'

'Your father?' And then Sarah laughed out loud.

And it was just then that her father came in smiling.

'What's the big joke? What are you two giggling about?'

And Sarah picked up the book and gave it to him. 'Just this silly book…'

And her father's face darkened – the light fled like sky darkening to a summer storm.

He threw it back on the bed.

'Filfth! That's what that is – filfth! You should be ashamed – both of you.'

Clarissa felt the last giggle still bubbling. 'Have you read it Dad?'

His face paled from dark red to cold white – pinched blue around his mouth and eyes. 'How dare you ask if I've read it!' and he left the room taking the brightness of the day with him.

And things had never really been the same after that.

Dad couldn't speak to her at all. He hardly even spoke to Mum at the table except things like 'ask Clarissa to please pass the butter'.

And Mum looked blotchy at breakfast, as if unpleasant things had happened at night.

Clarissa thought it would all blow over in a day or two, but each day turned worse than the one before – the silence took on the quality of sheet glass, so hard that when it broke the shards would draw blood.

Clarissa thought she might leave before someone was

mortally wounded.

If Dad knew about Jamie Oxley he'd have a heart attack – carrying on like this about a book for gods sake.

What would he do if he'd seen her and Jamie stark naked by the creek and Jamie with his willie sticking out like one of those hatpegs at school – it had been rather sweet really, but Dad wouldn't think that.

Never mind that nothing had really happened – it had been interesting, and kind of fun in an illegal sort of a way

But if Dad had seen them – well it just didn't bear thinking about. And if she stayed at home for much longer Dad was clearly going to turn into a problem – he wasn't going to change – you didn't need to be a genius to work that one out.

Mum had cried when she'd mentioned leaving home, but that was because Mum might have already seen that's what she'd have to do and there was nothing anyone could do to change things.

'You could go away to boarding school for your last two years.'

'No Mum – that would be just as bad as being here – worse.

'No, I'll go and stay with Aunty Joan at Manly – she's always saying come and live with her. I reckon I could be a day-girl at Manly and live with Aunty Joan.'

'She's always had a soft spot for you, my Joannie. I'd have to ring her.'

'Would you Mum? Would you?'

'Yes, well it'll probably break your father's heart, to say nothing of mine – but yes, I could ring her I suppose.'

Sarah brushed her nose.

'You'd have to promise me you wouldn't do anything silly darling – God knows Joannie was always the wild one in our family. I can't see her shortening the reins on you I'm afraid.'

'Oh Mum – you know me – half the time I'm frightened of my own shadow.'

'It's the other half that concerns me', said Sarah, but she had a bit of a smile when she said it.

God – it would be so wonderful to be free.

She'd have to tell Jamie.

And suddenly the thought of not seeing Jamie again cut like a sharp blade, somewhere deep.

***

'Dad's taking sheep to the Show on Sunday, Mum's going too – I hate the show, the flies and the dust and heat and the drunks at the bar tent – it's always the same ones, they look at you as you walk past – I told Mum I had homework.'

'I can get the truck – we could go down to the creek if you like.'

Clarissa nodded. 'Pick me up at the mailbox – don't come up to Windermere.'

'What time?'

'Eleven o'clock?'

'Okay.'

Her Mum and Dad had left with two ewes and a ram in the back of the ute at six in the morning – the day already an oven door slowly opening. Clarissa hadn't been able to write a word of revision to her essay – it all looked so stupid she didn't know why she'd bothered to write it in the first place.

She checked her maths, but there were no mistakes and by half past nine she was down at the mailbox sitting out of sight behind the big tree at the front gate. The flies gathered around her face, the oven door had opened wider and a smell of baked eucalyptus rose from the dead leaves she sat on.

Her mind was empty as a burst balloon.

When she looked at her watch again it was ten past ten.

At eleven o'clock what little movement there might have been in the air had completely stilled – cicadas rattled in the tree above her, grasshoppers clicked in the dry grass and flies gathered around her eyes. She could feel sweat collecting under her hat.

Eleven thirty and no Jamie – Clarissa wanted to stand up and walk home but she lacked the energy to move at all. She felt if she tried to move her legs they just wouldn't work so she stayed sitting against the trunk of the tree watching small black ants wind single file around her legs and up the tree. For some reason they chose not to walk over her feet – she'd have to move if they did.

'Dad said if I wasn't going to help with the cattle at the Show I could go out and check the pump in Big Scrubby – sorry I'm late.'

She hadn't heard the truck – Jamie's voice startled her.

'That's okay – I must have been asleep – Mum and Dad left at six with the precious sheep'. She giggled.

'We go down to the creek?'

Clarissa nodded – 'okay'.

It seemed closer this time – they passed three cars. 'Going to the Show I suppose' said Clarissa, and those were the only words spoken until the truck was deep in the acacias and coolabahs on the bend of the creek.

Clarissa followed Jamie through the trees to the creek bank, shed her clothes as he shed his and followed him running over the hot gravel into the brown water.

And this time things were quite different.

This time their bodies slid together like playful young seals – this time there was not a lot of talking – this time their bodies were having their say and they didn't need much in the way of words – just little sounds that might have been surprise and might have been acquiescence – questions that were answered before they were asked.

***

'I'm going to stay with my Auntie Joan in Manly – go to school down there.'

They were lying on their clothes spread on the smooth creek-gravel.

'Why?'

'Mostly because of Dad I suppose.'

'Why does he want you to go?'

'It's not him – it's me wants to go because of him.'

'What's he done?"

'Oh – he just doesn't want me to grow up – well not as a

girl, anyway. Probably be alright if I was a boy.' She giggled. 'I think he's frightened I'd do what we've just done.'

'You said you couldn't think of anything worse last time – you said you couldn't see how people ever got around to it.'

'I know – I know. But that was ages ago.'

'Yeah – like last week. D'you think you'll be okay?'

'How do you mean?'

Jamie looked down, scratched the gravel with a twig. 'I mean like babies and stuff.'

'You mean do I think I'm pregnant? God – I haven't any idea.'

'Could you be?'

'Well – technically – yes, I suppose so.'

'Jesus.'

'Well I mean that's how it happens after all – we all know that.'

'Yeah – but Jesus.'

'Jamie – I don't think it's very likely.'

Jamie looked up quickly. 'Don't you? Why not?'

'Well, it's the first time for a start.'

'I don't think that makes much difference.'

Clarissa could see Jamie was getting skittish – like a frightened colt – in a minute he would be on his feet putting on his clothes – and she wanted to prolong this moment.

'Yes well – I don't know about that – but anyway it's pretty late in the month for me.'

'How do you mean?'

'I mean I should know the awful truth in a couple of days – that's what I mean.'

'Oh – yeah. I see. D'you think it's okay then?'

Clarissa smiled at him – nodded. 'Yes – I think so' even though she had absolutely no idea. She tweaked his small pale nipple, ran her fingers down the washboard of his ribs.

'I think it's okay Jamie – I think it's safe' and she was amazed at how little she cared for the consequences, how much she wanted him to come back to her – to stay with her here on this sunbaked creek bank with only insects and birds to see them.

And even as Jamie's body reawakened she knew that this was their last time, that they would never be here again – she could feel Jamie's spirit pulling away from her even as their bodies were making their strange new magic.

It was slower this time – maybe it was Jamie's reluctance, but Clarissa had time to remember everything – and there was a moment when something almost happened – she could see the shock of it in his eyes – and then the thread snapped just like that, and it was over.

Jamie looked at his watch. 'Jesus – look at the time – it's five o'clock – they'll be leaving the showground,' and Jamie began to scrabble into his clothes.

Clarissa lay on the bank watching him.

'Come on Clarissa – your Mum and Dad will be home soon

– aren't you going to get dressed?'

Clarissa knew her mother would not leave until the cake and flower exhibits had all been packed away and taken back by the exhibitors – then Sarah would help tidy up the pavilion – she wouldn't get away till six – well maybe half past five at the earliest.

Clarissa lay naked on her dress, her body utterly boneless – watched Jamie squirm into his jeans.

'Come on Clarissa – get dressed,' and Jamie dragged her to her feet and she flopped against him and giggled, as much at his alarm as anything.

He pulled her singlet over her arms, down over her head, lifted her feet one by one into her undies and tugged them up her legs – but in the end she relented, shrugged into her dress, put on her socks and shoes.

'Okay' she said, looking at Jamie. 'Now what?'

And she already knew the answer to that question – had known it from the moment she lowered the backs of her legs onto the prickles of horsehair poking through the seat of Jamie's old truck.

She was making a baby – she could feel the fire of new life growing inside her at this very moment.

Clarissa laughed at the absurdity of the idea.

'What's the joke?' And then without waiting for an answer – 'we don't get home before your parents it won't be so funny.'

And Clarissa looked at him and she put a hand on his arm and smiled – 'oh Jamie, Jamie,' and shook her head.

As if her parents knowing she had been with Jamie could

possibly make the slightest difference to the spark of life kindling within her.

The logical part of her mind and its recent biology lessons told her that Jamie's eager little sperms probably hadn't even yet reached the egg she sheltered deep in the fastness of her womb – an egg ripe for such an encounter, no matter what she had told Jamie.

But on a deeper, intuitive layer she was certain such a union of sperm and egg had already taken place – she could practically feel the eager little tadpole wriggling its way through the soft and receptive shell of her own large fat egg – forming the first cell of new life – and then beginning to divide in the extravagant joy of creating a new human being.

But Jamie wasn't fatherhood material – Jamie wanted only to be rid of her before her parents came home.

Ah well – now she really had a reason to go and live with Aunty Joan at Manly. The thought of exposing a gradually distending belly to Dad's Calvinistic gaze simply did not live.

Once she was at Manly with Aunty Joan some solution would present itself.

'Okay Jamie – let's go and climb in that rattly old truck – but I want your shirt to sit on.'

'What for? I can't go driving around without a shirt. What if someone sees us?'

'Okay then – I'll sit on mine.'

'Jesus – Alright, take mine – but why?'

'That seat's so prickly it's going to give me a rash all down the backs of my legs – then there will be some explaining.'

Clarissa didn't really think she'd get a rash, but she liked the idea of sitting on Jamie's shirt – and besides, a little bit of disquiet wouldn't do him any harm.

The shirt was cool and damp against her newly tender skin. She smiled at Jamie.

'Okay?'

She nodded.

'I'll want it back before we get to your place – or a car comes.'

Clarissa didn't think it was worth making a reply.

DICK AND JANE

Right from the start Bill said 'Jesus Dick – a fucken redheaded woman is trouble – pick a blonde or a brunette – not a fucken redhead. She'll just make you miserable boy – it's a known fucken fact. Fucken redheads are nothing but grief!'

But then Bill says pretty much the same thing about any beer that isn't Fourex.

Anyway I was already too far into green eyes that promised I don't know what –

And that mouth – lips so full and red I just yearned, pale skin so fragile it might tear at any moment – bloodvessels beating so close beneath they were like roadmaps.

And the hair.

Well I just loved the hair – bright as polished copper in the sunshine, dark and thick as blood at night, writhing like a nest of snakes around her head.

As if I could say no – as if I had any choice.

Of course right from the start there were moments when things inside Jane would boil to the surface –

'I saw you looking at Libby's tits – don't shake your head like that – I saw you you lecherous bastard. How can I ever trust you?'

Libby had nice tits – Libby had great tits, and maybe I sneaked a look.

Well of course I did. What man wouldn't? But more than that? No way.

And then Jane would subside as quickly as she'd erupted and things would be fine again – things would be just so much more than fine than anyone outside the two of us could ever conceive. Things would be absolfuckinglutely glorious.

Until little Nell came along.

Jane didn't want Nell – not ever, although she made out she did some of the time – but it was a pretty uncomfortable pregnancy. She was sick, her skin the blue white of skim milk, her hair beetroot and old seaweed lying dark on her skin.

A forest of blue worms grew behind her knees, ran down her legs – I could see them wriggle their way down a little more each day.

Jane hated those worms, hated her swollen vomiting body, hated the cold clamminess of her skin, hated me for putting the baby inside her.

And when Nell was born Jane wanted nothing to do with her.

I've seen a cow kick her newborn calf away from her udder, not let it near her to suck – kick it away until it died.

That's what Jane was like with Nell.

I mean she didn't hit her or push her away or anything, but Jane didn't like Nell sucking her either – I could see that as clearly as if she had kicked her. She didn't like Nell near her nipples – the matron tried to get her to use a breast pump; 'stimulate your milk dear – ' but Jane looked at the breast pump as if it was someone's idea of a joke, in very poor taste.

Once they weaned Nell onto that formula milk things settled down – and in spite of everything Nell had a week of Jane's colostrum and stuff so it could have been worse.

Well of course later on it was worse – much worse, but back then once Nell took to the formula I remember thinking things would be okay.

Sure they were okay – that's why Jane's doing five to seven years in the womens' correctional centre on the Central Coast and little Nell wears a patch over one eye and walks with a limp.

Although you have to look pretty closely to notice the limp these days, and Doc Halliday says he thinks he might be able to save twenty five percent of the sight in the eye.

Anyway, Nell's gone to stay with little Zoey Long from her pre school – she's mad about Zoey and Susie Long said she'd just love to have Nell for the night so here I am driving back to our empty house and thinking thank god Jane's where she can't do anyone any harm for a few years.

What's going to happen when she gets out I just don't want to think about.

Jasmine the cat isn't around when I open the door. Jasmine's a Siamese with more of a moan than a purr – and she does wander a bit, although she's usually waiting to get in when I come home.

Jasmine never did like Jane, not from the first moment, and I guess the feeling was mutual. Jasmine just used to disappear when Jane was around, although she's been much more domestic this last year I must say.

My gut told me Jane was going to freak out with little Nell one day and I ignored my gut instincts – you should never do that – so often they're all you've got. I mean ignore them and who the fuck are you going to listen to?

Your careers councillor?

Cardinal Pell?

George W Bush?

Anyway – yeah – I ignored my gut instincts and next thing you know on her third birthday party Nell spills raspberry syrup on Jane's new blouse and Jane takes to her with a toy cricket bat.

I was in the kitchen lighting the candles on the cake and all the kids are suddenly screaming and little Nell's lying on her back on the table white as death itself and this blood coming out of her ear and Jane's got the cricket bat in one hand and she's brushing at her blouse with the other and she's shaking – shaking with rage and I don't know who to go for – Jane and the bat or little Nell and then Jane looks down at her and Nell moves a tiny bit and Jane raises the bat and so it's Jane.

God she's strong.

It's like grabbing a lioness – all muscle and teeth and claws and she goes for my eyes with the bat in a hard flat swing and I grab it and I hear bones break but I hang on – I mean if I let go now Nell's next and all the kids are screaming and some of the mothers grab Jane from behind and gradually they get her down and quieter and I pick up little Nell and one leg flops like a broken doll and someone's called the ambulance and the police and oh Jesus.

Three years old and she's like a dog that's been run over by a car, except she's not making any noise.

Well it's taken a year to get her back to where she is now

– the nurses were wonderful – 'amazing girl' they said and Nell kept asking for Mummy – 'Mummy's sick too' she'd say. 'Mummy's sick too', and she was more right than she could ever know.

I let myself into the house and pour myself a brandy and dry which is something I never do and I collapse on the couch and don't even turn the news on – just sit, not even thinking really – and I see Jasmine's tail poking out behind the TV. Blue-grey with a black tip, and it's lying there like a sock full of sand.

The telephone rings – it's Susie Long and my heart freezes.

'No Nell's fine – she and Zoey have finally fallen asleep in the same bed. No Dick I just wondered if you'd seen the news – three women escaped from that place on the central coast, coming back from treatment – they think the bus driver will be okay – no they didn't give names.'

PENSION PLAN

Agricultural Research and Supply Enterprises gave Frank Stanthorpe, BSc.Ag., the boot thirteen months before the Pension Plan was due to kick in.

Of course they didn't call it giving him the boot, they called it strategic downsizing in the interests of ongoing workplace efficiencies.

Frank had seen it coming ever since they shut down the Agronomy research labs and the extension services. Frank had worked for A.R.S.E. for twenty nine years, lived through all the jokes, dragged his family through a dozen dusty outback towns, some little more than a one room school, two churches and three pubs.

Two years to a project – long enough to make acquaintances, not long enough to make friends – dragging Hilda and the kids over dirt roads dry grass and dying trees beyond the great divide – watching towns shrink and wither, watching the Department of Agriculture services dwindle away until they vanished.

Any fool could see country towns were in a bad way, losing ground ever since the Korean War, when wool took the first king hit from Nylon and Dacron. By the time the drought hit in 1965 the writing was on the wall for anyone who bothered to read it.

Oh there'd been a couple of bounces in wheat – lasted just long enough to catch all the farmers who bought bright new yellow machines – a couple of good years in cattle, and then it all went on sliding right down the drain, taking a whole new bunch of suckers with it.

When the kids finished primary school they'd sent them to live with Louise, Hilda's sister in Balmain for their secondary schooling. Louise was easy with Aileen, their oldest, although Jack showed more interest than Frank liked.

By the time Brian went to stay Aileen was in third year and Jack made it known that more money would not go astray. A lot more. Jeffrey followed Brian three years later, emptying both Frank's house and his wallet.

But getting the kids an education was the deal. Twenty years ago Frank had abandoned hopes of becoming CEO of Agricultural Resource and Supply Enterprises, fifteen years ago he'd given up on General Manager, five years ago he'd settled on Regional Manager and hung on for the Pension Plan.

Now this – shat out by the big ARSE thirteen months short of the money.

Frank owned the caravan and his car, a Ford Falcon with a shudder in the steering that felt expensive and a whine in the diff that he didn't want to think about. Hilda owned a cottage back in the hills behind Gosford left to her by her parents. The tenants had stuffed the stove and taken the fridge, the house was fibro and Frank wondered should they pull it down – rebuild. Were there grants for that sort of thing? No grants, they couldn't afford it. In the meantime they'd paint it and live there, hope the asbestos didn't get them.

But what were they going to do for money? The kids were all through school now, Aileen and Jeffrey had finished University – Aileen working in Hospitality and Jeffrey in Communications. Frank was buggered if he could see how you could make money out of either of them, but that was no longer his problem.

Brian was a plumber, end up richer than the lot of them, support his parents into the bargain, most likely.

But not yet.

In the meantime, how the fuck were he and Hilda going to live?

'You could grow some of that Marijuana,' said Hilda.

You never knew what Hilda was likely to come up with. Frank looked at her.

'Don't look at me like that. Why not? It's worth thousands a plant Ethel says– and I mean, after all, you are an Ag Scientist aren't you?'

Hilda had grown fond of quoting Ethel, ran the hair salon downtown. Knew it all, made up the rest.

Frank nodded. 'Have to be hydroponics.'

'Why?'

'So you can hide it.'

'That means a lot of electricity for the lights doesn't it? That's what Ethel says – her Leanne told her you've got to start right away when you move into a new flat – else you'll get a big spike in the electricity when you turn the big lights on. They watch for that sort of thing.'

'This Leanne grows it does she?'

'Yes, well I don't know – says you've got to watch the pH – goes too high all the plants turn male, loose their heads. Says the heads are the good parts. Cut the plants at three months, hang them up to dry then cut off the heads. That's what Ethel's Leanne says.'

'Sounds like Ethel talks too much for her own good,' said Frank.

'Don't say things like that about my friends – I'm only trying to help you know. I mean it was you got the sack, not me.'

'You've got nothing to get the sack from.' Hilda looked a bit hurt. 'But yes, you're right – Ethel's right – Leanne's right. You need a lot of electricity for hydroponics. Two thousand watts of light will grow two, three plants max. And you need an alfoil lined cupboard, fans, pumps, tubs, the lot.

'I reckon to grow twenty plants you'd need fifteen to twenty thousand watts.'

'Sounds expensive,' said Hilda. 'Still, if it's worth all that money, it'd be worthwhile wouldn't it?'

'Depends,' said Frank.

'Depends on what?'

'If you can sell it.'

'Oh Frank – don't be so negative. Have faith. Of course you can sell it. I'll sell it. You grow it – I'll sell it. More tea?'

Never been much of a one for faith, Frank hadn't. Faith was for fools too lazy to work things out for themselves. Look where faith in the big A.R.S.E. had got him – faith in the face of common sense and his better judgement. A sea of shit. That's where faith had got him. Shit two feet deep and him on the bones of his arse in the middle of it.

Well fuck the lot of them – if they could do that to a bloke like him they could do it to anyone – and they deserved just exactly whatever he chose to ram up their collective arses in return.

In this case it wasn't anything very complicated – just a simple agricultural operation cultivating a little hash, hemp, grass, Mary Jane, whatever – *Cannabis sativa.*

It wasn't a hard plant to grow – Ethel's Leanne was right about the pH – what they paid big money for were those big rich heads the female plants put out. But there was a market for the leaf.

The knowledge came with his job – Frank hadn't gone looking for it, but he'd picked up a lot more than he realised over a lifetime in the field and the labs.

Matter of fact Roger Jameison in agronomy research had a nice little plant selection program going, Cannabis with high level THC, tucked away in a corner of one of the labs where nobody went much. Roger had shown him a couple of years ago. Roger smoked the stuff. Frank had no interest in smoking it, just growing and selling it.

Roger said the best technique was propagation by cuttings from proven high performance plants. He had seeds as well, but Frank reckoned he'd try the cuttings first up. Pity he couldn't grow it out in the sunshine.

Frank remembered the small sweet strawberries from his mother's garden. Not like the supermarket hydroponic strawberries today, puffed up five times the size they should be, full of air, popped like soggy balloons when you bit them, tasted like soap. He hoped his *Cannabis sativa* didn't come out like those strawberries.

Frank had the wiring of the old cottage checked out. On its own at the end of Cypress lane and half a kilometre of unpaved street, one streetlight, the cottage was served by a 5KVA transformer. The electrician pulled out a couple of switches to check the wiring.

'That's fucking asbestos mate, I'm not getting up in that fucking roof. Anyway the wiring's crap, old.'

He looked at Frank, about to say more and stopped.

'You'd be lucky to run a fucking stove and a toaster without burning the place down.'

'Maybe the asbestos'd put the fire out,' said Frank.

'Better you than me mate. It was me, I'd pull the whole heap of shit down, build a new house, brick veneer, steel frame – get council to put in one of those new 50 KVA transformers.'

He spat.

'You can't do diddlysquat with what you got here.'

Frank could see the hydroponics had to go. Hide in Plain Sight. Wasn't that the title of something? But Frank had just remembered that extraordinary book *My Six Convicts.*

Written by a prison psychiatrist, there was a guy in that book that could quieten a whole screaming psychiatric prison ward just by entering it.

That had nothing to do with why the book leapt into his mind, but still, it was something that had caught in his memory.

***

'Place looks nice Frank,' said Constable Jim Carruthers, otherwise known as Jum in the Gosford RSL, where Frank spent the occasional half hour at the end of the day. 'See you've been doing a bit of gardening.'

'Yep – now I'm not going off to work each day, Hilda says I might as well help out in the garden.'

'What you got growing there?'

'Fruit trees – oranges, apples, mandarins, grapefruit. Can't stand grapefruit myself, but Hilda wanted them.. And of course the figs were already there,' pointing at four large fig trees beside a winding ornamental hedge.

'Vegetables?'

'Yep – carrots, tomatoes, peas – planted a few pots of strawberries.'

'Yeah – those supermarket strawberries taste like fruit-flavoured kapok don't they?'

Frank smiled, nodded.

'What's that hedge you got there?' pointing at the dark green plants, palmate leaves, winding around the paths, bordering the vegetable plots, separating the orchard from the rest of the garden.

Frank looked at it – shrugged. 'God knows, something Hilda found in one of her gardening magazines – South America I think.'

'I like them roses,' said Jum. 'I grow roses, the wife says they look like a bunch of sticks half the year – why bother? But I like them – so does she when they bloom.'

'Yep,' Frank nodded. 'We've got Peace, Washington Pinks, Just Joey – dunno what half of them are called.'

Jum nodded again. 'Well, better be moving on – take care.'

'You too Jum, see you around.' Frank watched him go, turned back to survey his garden.

It had passed the first test.

In *My Six Convicts* the author described how he persuaded the Warden of the Jail to allow the inmates to garden as a form of therapy. The inmates had planted ornamental hedges bordering all of the prison walkways, planted flowerbeds inside them.

The state Corrective Services Board visited the prison en masse, complimented the Warden on his progressive prisoner rehabilitation program. The Warden smirked graciously.

The hedges were *Cannabis sativa*, and escaped detection from first sprout until just before harvest, when the Warden's career suffered a sharp reversal.

Anyway – now the project had received its first (unofficial) tick of approval in the person of Jum, Constable first class Jim Carruthers. Maybe the way ahead would not be without its little problems – but the thing was, Frank was of an age when no one – absolutely no one – was going to suspect him of growing happy weed, so who was going to check on him?

Still, it mightn't be a bad idea to have a bird net or something that he could draw over his hedges like a sort of camouflage net should the need arise.

He'd do that, just in case. Drape it over the fruit trees – especially the figs, and just sort of let it hang over the hedges when the plants got taller. He might need to trim them, to alleviate the look they got at a certain size, but he had no doubt the clippings themselves would be valuable.

The THC levels might not be so high in plants out in the sunlight drawing nutrients from the soil the way nature intended. He'd have to check on that. But it was sure as shit a lot safer in the long run than turning the place upside down for hydroponics.

That summer Frank trimmed his hedges every week, raked the clippings, kept them in those white woven bags A.R.S.E. used for packaging seeds and fertilizer. If anyone saw him raking the hedge clippings they didn't say anything. And besides, the nearest neighbour was three hundred metres away.

By December Frank had ten white bags stored in the garden shed – stuffed full of hedge clippings. Frank rang his daughter Aileen, tried in a roundabout way to discover if she knew anyone who might be interested in buying his clippings, but Aileen missed it.

'Jesus Dad – I haven't done any of that stuff for years. Stop worrying about me! Get a life!' And she hung up.

He rang his son Jeffrey in communications, but Jeffrey was overseas.

He rang Brian, the plumber.

'Sure Dad, see what I can do. The guys suck on a bit of weed now and again – I'll get back to you.'

***

'This shit's no fucking good mate – couldn't get rid of it if I sent it as drought relief to starving fucking cows.'

The speaker was Victor Morales, small and dark and oily – he looked Mediterranean and his Australian accent was broader than Frank's.

'It's all like old dry shit, see – no fresh buds in it, no heads. You ain't got no heads, you ain't got jack shit.'

Victor shook his head.

'Tell ya what – I'll give you five bucks a fucking bag and I'm doing you a favour at that.'

Victor was Brian's contact. Brian had kept away.

'Two hundred dollars the lot,' said Frank. He'd secretly been hoping for a thousand dollars for his clippings.

'Mate, you've got to be having a loan of yourself. Sure you ain't been smoking this shit?' Victor kicked the bags again.

'Tell ya what – favour to Brian I'll give you a hundred bucks for the ten bags.'

'Hundred and fifty' said Frank.

'Shit! I must be going soft in the head. Okay mate, hundred and fifty. Give us a hand to load them in the ute will ya?'

***

'Not bad for a few hedge clippings,' said Frank, waving the wad of dirty ten dollar bills under Hilda's nose in the kitchen.

'That's nice dear,' said Hilda.

Victor Morales wholesaled the lot for $1000 a bag that afternoon, bragged about it in the pub that night. Brian overheard.

'Dad, that little spic, Morales, what'd he pay you for that stuff?'

'Fifteen dollars a bag. He offered me five, I got him up to fifteen.'

'Greasy little bastard, skiting he sold it for a grand a bag last night.'

'Jesus!' said Frank. 'Well, that's just the first cut, won't make that mistake again.'

Victor turned up at the back gate two weeks later.

'Found a feller took that stuff of me hands – didn't make nothing on it, but he might be looking for a bit more when ya got some.'

Frank looked at Victor, nodded slowly. 'I'll have five bags Saturday.'

'Okay – yeah. Saturday, got me dogs running Saturday out Wagga way – might call round Monday or Tuesday if I got time.'

Frank nodded again. 'See you Tuesday then, five thirty.'

'Five thirty it is,' said Victor.

Five thirty Tuesday Victor's ute pulled in beside the garden shed. Brian and Frank stepped out as Victor climbed out of his ute.

'Ripped my old man off, didn't you Vic. Couldn't help yourself.'

'Waddya mean? I got lucky is all – coulda been stuck with that shit forever just as likely. Anyway, I only got me costs back.'

'That's not what I heard.'

'What the fuck would you know, mate?'

'Heard you in the pub that night mate – heard you skiting

about getting a grand a bag from some old fool you'd paid fifteen bucks a bag to.'

'Well what if I fucking did?'

'Half that belongs to the old man – that's what.'

A sharp sliver of blade grew from nowhere out of Victor's hand, but the Stillson in Brian's fist was already on its way, the heavy toothed pipe wrench caught Victor's wrist – snapped it with the dull click of breaking chalk.

'Half of it mate – now.'

'Ah – fuck!' Victor paled as the pain flowered in his wrist. 'What the fuck ya do that for?'

'Don't like someone ripping off the old man Victor. Pay him. Five grand.'

'Ain't got the money.'

Brian, twice the size of Victor, shifted the Stillson in his hand.

'Okay – okay – it's in the glovebox.'

Brian followed him to the ute, stood by the door as Victor bent, rummaged in the car with his good hand. When he straightened up he was holding a revolver. An old revolver, the nickel plating peeling off the end of the barrel. It wobbled in Victor's hand, but Brian could see the dull gleam of bullets in the open chambers.

'Shit!' Brian backed away.

'Ya broke me fucking wrist, ya prick.'

'Don't shoot – put it down.'

'Put them fucking bags in the ute and shut up.'

Vic turned to Frank. 'Get me some fucking strapping for me wrist.'

Frank scrambled towards the house.

Vic yelled at him. 'Don't try anything smart – like calling the cops.'

Frank burst into the house.

'Hilda – give me a roll of sticky bandage or something. And call the police – quick!'

Frank emerged a minute later with an Elastoplast bandage.

'Strap me wrist up – Jesus fucking Christ be careful – oh fuck.'

Vic paled, his knees sagged, he collapsed on the ground.

'Grab the gun' said Frank, but Brian already had it.

'What the fuck do we do now?' asked Brian.

Hilda appeared on the back porch. 'The police are on their way' she said. 'They asked me what was happening – I had to say I didn't know, just that Frank said it was an emergency.'

'Get the bags back in the shed Brian – quick.'

Frank and Brian unloaded the white bags from the back of the ute, stuffed them in the shed, locked the door.

A police siren made its little dying burble as the car pulled up in a dazzle of blue and red flashes beside Victor's ute. Two uniformed police officers climbed out, one of them Jum Carruthers.

'Hullo Frank, Brian – what's going on? Where's the emergency?'

Frank pointed at Vic on the ground. 'Right here – this little bastard came at us with a knife, Brian got him with the wrench, broke his wrist. Then he pulled a gun – keeled over while Hilda was calling you.'

'Who is he?'

'Never seen him before in my life,' said Frank.

Brian shook his head.

'What's he doing here with a knife and a gun?' the second officer asked. He had sergeant's chevrons on his sleeve.

Frank shrugged. 'Wrong address?'

The sergeant had taken possession of the revolver and was peering into Victor's face.

'I know this bastard – he's a small time drug pusher. You fellers into happy weed?' He was smiling as he said that.

Frank shook his head, grinning himself. 'Do I look like it?'

'What about you mate?' to Brian.

'I'm too busy for that sort of shit,' said Brian.

'Mind if I take a look around?' said the sergeant. Frank didn't really think no was an option.

'Go ahead, Hilda's inside, knock on the door first would you.'

The sergeant disappeared into the house, emerged a few minutes later – rattled the door of the garden shed. 'What's in here?'

'Nothing, go on in.' Frank undid the padlock.

'What's in these bags?'

'Hedge clippings.' Frank opened one, dipped in a hand, pulled out a handful of dried twigs and leaves, let them trickle back into the bag. 'Going to compost them when I get a bin set up.'

Frank and the two policemen strolled around the garden, admired the trim hedges, the fruit trees. Frank offered them some figs.

'Thanks Frank,' said Jum.

'We'll take this bloke in – get to the bottom of it soon enough,' said the sergeant. 'You fellows come down later and sign a statement, okay?'

Vic had regained consciousness, Hilda had torn an old sheet for a sling, they sat him tight-lipped and pale in the back, the sergeant beside him. Frank and Brian watched Jum back out the driveway.

Brian shook his head. 'Jesus Dad – that was close.'

'Not over yet, son.'

Brian looked at him. 'You reckon Vic'll talk?'

'I don't know – but there's worse things than talking.'

***

The police returned the following morning armed with a search warrant.

'Sorry about this Frank – that little wop says he bought ten bags of hash off you a couple of weeks ago. We've got to search the place properly.'

'Go ahead,' said Frank.

'Where's Brian?'

Frank shrugged, 'Working.'

'Okay,' said the sergeant, 'let's see those bags in the shed for a start.'

Frank pointed to a smouldering pile down the gully behind the shed, ash and dead gum leaves around the margins.

'You burnt them? Thought you were going to compost them.'

'Next time,' said Frank.

'You got a permit for that fire?'

Frank nodded. 'Rang Council yesterday, Health and Building officer George Healy. Gave me permission, sending the permit.'

The sergeant strode angrily away around the block of land, peering in the gully, in scrubby corners.

'Who's your mate?' Frank said to Jum.

'Sore Arsehole,' Jum smiled. 'Detective Sergeant Saul Aspinall – hotshot down from Sydney. Sorry about him – I knew that little Vic was lying, but Sore Arsehole goes and gets a warrant, and here we are. Good a way to waste time as any I guess.'

Detective Sergeant Aspinall returned from his tour of the yard, the gardens.

'Like some more figs?' said Frank.

'Thanks Frank, the missus really liked those ones yesterday.'

'Fuck the figs!' said Aspinall. 'We're not taking any fucking figs.'

Jum shrugged.

'Suit yourself,' said Frank.

***

'The pension plan's looking a bit dodgy,' Frank said to Hilda after the police had gone.

'Don't be discouraged dear – I'm sure you'll work something out. The garden looks so nice, especially that dear little hedge. You give Jum some figs?'

Frank shook his head. 'His boss wouldn't let him take them. Who was it said "corruption begins with the first cigar"? He should have said with the first fig.'

'Oh well, he'll get over it – you'll just have to be more careful next time dear – find another buyer.'

'Think I better find someone who lives a long way from here – like Brisbane or Melbourne or something.'

'That's a good plan dear. How're you going to do that?'

Frank shook his head. 'No idea.'

'There's always my sister Mavis and her Bill in Perth you know.'

'Mavis and Bill? What possible use could they be? Bill's just retired from the Bank hasn't he? What would he know?'

'Well, Mavis used to smoke a bit of stuff when she was young – I remember being so shocked, but she never gave it a thought. Wouldn't be surprised if she still smokes a bit – she could easily know someone over there.'

***

Frank managed to fit twenty four bags into the caravan – it didn't leave much room for him and Hilda and it took them six days to get to Perth. But Bill had it all pre-sold by the time they got there.

Six hundred dollars a bag.

He gave Bill a hundred dollars a bag – Bill didn't want to take it at first, but Frank said 'I'll have another couple of loads later in the year mate, this thing could get bigger – I wouldn't feel happy if you didn't get a cut.'

Detective Sergeant Aspinall called on Frank and Hilda the week they got home, Jum Carruthers following a pace or two behind.

'Feel I should warn you – word is there's someone coming after you – don't know who, don't know when. But that's the word.'

'Why?' said Frank.

'That stuff you never grew, never sold I guess,' said Aspinall. 'That feller we took in, Victor Morales, he's been making a lot of noise, he'll be out soon – I'd be thinking twice about things if I were you.'

'I will,' said Frank. 'I will. Meanwhile – what are you doing about it?'

Aspinall shook his head. 'Nothing mate, nothing. What can I do? You've done nothing, Morales has done nothing – nobody's done anything. Just telling you for your own good, that's all.'

Frank stayed silent – looked at the fig tree now bare of fruit – looked at the dark green hedges, looked at Jum Carruthers. Jum shrugged.

'Unless of course you want to tell me what this is really all about,' said Aspinall.

'I don't know any more than you,' said Frank. 'Probably not as much.'

Aspinall turned away and spat. 'Right then – make it hard for us you just make it harder for yourself.'

And they left.

***

Frank and Hilda and the caravan went to Perth twice more that year – each time they managed to pack thirty bags into the caravan.

'We should sell the house Frank, buy one in Perth. Mavis says there's a nice one for sale in her street.'

'Maybe we should sell this one,' said Frank. 'But we shouldn't buy one in Perth, not if that's our market. Brisbane maybe, or Adelaide.'

'Brisbane would be nice – on the coast somewhere.'

Frank cut the hedge down, replanted with giant privet, sold the house and made the trip to Perth with the dried hedge plants occupying the entire caravan. They stayed in motels all the way, including one with rude dolls half way across the Nullarbor. He was getting tired of driving on a road whose gutters were lined with the bloated bodies of dead kangaroos, bottles and tins glinting in the sunset.

That trip netted them twenty thousand dollars.

What with the money from the caravan trips and the sale of the house they had enough money to buy a nice house with a pool and five acres in the hills behind Byron Bay. From the house they had a view of the lighthouse, and all the way up the coast to the blurred outlines of the Gold Coast High-rises.

Frank was in two minds about re-planting at Byron, but Hilda said 'Why not?' so Frank planted a hedge down both sides of the long winding driveway.

Frank took to spending an hour in the evenings in the Bangalow RSL, met Arthur (Australia Taxation Office - retired) and Rupert (Australian Federal Police - retired), both of them his age, smart, capable – bored shitless.

'There's enough brainpower in this place to run the United Nations three times over and give you change,' said Frank one day.

'Wouldn't be hard,' said Arthur. 'What you got in mind, Frank?'

'Grey power – there's a few of us around with plenty of savvy and nothing to do – we could form a co-operative of all the Cannabis growers up here, market it, transport it, the lot.'

'How would you market it?' said Arthur.

'Capital cities,' said Rupert. 'Stay out of the little towns, too easy to trace – go with the big cities.'

Frank nodded. 'Could you do that, Rupert?'

'I reckon I could. Yeah.'

'I can give you Perth,' said Frank.

'Good,' said Rupert. 'What about transport?'

'Caravans' said Frank. 'There's thousands of caravans out there drifting around Australia, driven by people just like us, nothing to do, time on their hands. Pay them a hundred bucks a bag, give them ten bags to deliver, thousand dollars cash – a lot of people would jump at it.'

'That's not as silly as it sounds,' said Arthur.

'Wasn't meant to sound silly' said Frank'

'I can do the finance,' said Arthur. 'Got to be careful how you wash it.'

'Wash what?' Asked Rupert.

'Wash the cash, launder it so it's legitimate.'

'Can you do that?' Frank this time.

'Sure – most people think it's all casinos, betting on racehorses and the dogs. A lot of hot cash finds its way there right enough. But there's other ways if you know how. You see in the past the Channel Islands….'

Frank cut him off.

'Arthur – if you can do it, that's fine. Don't tell me about it – I don't want to know. I'll do production and transport. Rupert'll handle marketing, you'll be our finance man.'

Arthur nodded. 'Okay – what'll we call ourselves? Rupert, Frank and Arthur? RAF? FAR?

'FAROUT' said Rupert.

'Farside,' said Frank, and Farside it was.

***

Farside became an unsung legend, no AGM, no annual balance sheet, no Annual Report, but for the three partners Farside netted five million dollars the first year. Cash.

The growers were all paid cash on delivery. Quality control was strict. Slip up once, no second chance. Farside doubled the price to growers in the second year and production doubled, profits trebled.

Fleets of caravans carried Farside merchandise around Australia, caravans towed by elderly couples going about their innocent retirement vacations. Farside enriched petrol stations, caravan parks, motels, bookmakers, TAB agencies, casinos, tourist centres, massage parlours, roadside cafes, to say nothing of pensioners and hobby farmers on the North Coast. Grower prices doubled again.

Hilda, with Denise and Barbara, the wives of Rupert and Arthur, set up a business importing Tibetan Artefacts, selling them in Bangalow, Byron Bay, Lismore. Hilda discovered she had a gift for administration.

They bought franchises in Casino, Lismore Bellingen, MacDonalds, Big Rooster, Kentucky Fried. They bought a hotel in Byron Bay.

Last time anyone looked, Farside profits exceeded thirty million dollars.

Cash.

INEZ

I saw her as soon as I entered the dance-hall – eyes bright, eager, dark hair, pink and white dress with black velvet ribbon – whitest teeth widening her smile – her eyes caught mine and I didn't see anyone else.

I hadn't wanted to go to the dance that marked some anniversary of my old Prep school – I had finished Senior school now – I was on my way to University, Prep schools were kid stuff. The dance was in the old dining room – it seemed a lot smaller –the girls from the nearby girls' school, sisters of boys, old-boys.

Her name was Inez, 'I think Mum was frightened by an Argentinian,' and I smiled although I had no idea what she was talking about. She was fifteen – younger than the others but her brother was captain of the school and she'd got a special ticket – I was just sixteen myself, I was used to being the youngest too. And over there was her sister Lucy, she was going to be Captain of the School next year. I'd never even been a sub-prefect.

Inez was as tall as the other girls, and every bit as womanly, but she couldn't dance to save herself. I liked foxtrots and quicksteps – I could dance – but she had this bumpy way of moving to the music – it didn't coincide with the rhythm or the tune or anything else – but it didn't matter in the slightest – it just made our journey around the floor a bit erratic.

We had a lot to say to each other, but the words came slowly. We made huge use of the words we found, and our smiles ached in place of words.

Our eyes danced, our eyes laughed, our eyes said things our lips could not manage, touched in ways our bodies dared not.

But something had happened.

'I think it's time you two found others to dance with.'

This large woman with the determined chin was her mother – and where Inez's eyes were huge, her mother's were small – but she had that well-corseted appearance of one accustomed to being obeyed. She smiled to soften her words, and it was a nice enough smile, but it lasted no longer than was absolutely necessary.

There was no shortage of partners for the girl in the pink and white dress – and I knew down to the exact nail in the floorboards where she was in the room for every note of the next six dances.

We pretended surprise when we came together again – her mother had gone – Lucy gave us a conspiratorial smile – Lucy was quite a big girl herself, in a blue dress, with her mother's eyes and her sister's smile – Lucy was my friend from the start.

And in the foxtrot and the quickstep a girl and a boy are meant to hold each other close. Inez still bumped and lurched out of time to the music, but already we dwelt within an unspoken conspiracy – I don't think either of us knew why, or where it might lead, we just knew conspiracy was vital.

At some time in the night there was this boy, tall and blond, resplendent in his school uniform – red striped navy trousers, grey jacket with silver buttons and red epaulettes of rank.

'This is Richard – Richard's repeating school to be Captain of Cadets.'

Repeating school.

Eight years of boarding school and I couldn't imagine anyone wanting to repeat.

Richard had a clear idea of his own worth – he was not sure if he would shake my hand – in the end it was a crushing grip. A grip that said things about territorial rights and the unsuitability of some people and wait until we meet on the football field – and Inez smiled at me as if Richard was on another planet – which he might well have been – he was not on ours.

Next day we watched the hockey match between my old prep school and Inez's school. The girls were quite a bit bigger than the boys and you could tell they were taking it a bit easy, and that was a mistake. In the end it was Inez flying down the wing – tunic thumping – who scored the equalizing goal, restoring some measure of honour.

The younger girls worshipped her.

She came up to me on the sideline, chest heaving, flashing that smile, eyes alight, cheeks flushed, the air between us full of unspoken promises.

'Great game,' I said.

'Inez has broken up with Richard – she does nothing but talk about you – forgive me for writing this but if you feel like writing her a letter I know she would love it. Only if you want to. Love, Lucy.'

The letter was written in pencil on a page torn from an exercise book in a big round hand that I would come to know.

I wrote to Inez that night – *I enjoyed the dance, you played hockey really well* – but somehow Inez managed to read significance into it.

***

Inez and Lucy are coming to stay with us at the beach. Their stay will be this weekend, the last of their school holidays, four glorious days, carefully timed to make allowance for Crutching. My older brother Simon and I are working in the shearing shed at home for Crutching – he as woolpresser, myself as board-boy.

Crutching will be good for us.

It is a time when wool is worth a pound a pound, and sheep are treated with veneration verging on idolatry. Up until now my life has been boarding-school bleakness broken by brief holidays at home and the rule of sheep.

On Wednesday it begins to rain – you can't crutch wet sheep – and we must stay home over the weekend to shed the sheep.

There are five stands – five shearers each man crutching a hundred head a run, two thousand sheep a day. The board boys sweep the board, keep the wool free of dags and maggots, pick up the wool with hinged boards or the folded cap from a jute woolpack, take the wool to the sorting table, run the tarpot at the call of *tarboy* to a sheep with flystrike or cuts – the tar these days is a chemical preparation called KFM – Kills Flies and Maggots – and it does.

Board-boys also help with the penning up – shearers must never run out of sheep – and help the woolpresser when the bins are overfull. It's busy enough, and it's started to rain and John, the other board boy, reaches for the boards at the same time as I do and he's a little bigger than me and he hangs on because the boards are easier to use than the folded woolpack cap.

He's a nice enough bloke John, but visions of Inez and the weekend that will no longer happen fill my head and I punch him.

I'm neither muscular nor large, but even Simon who is half again as big as me has learnt to avoid unnecessary fights.

'Right youse two!' It's George, the overseer – 'Outside – get ya shirts an shoes off – get stuck inna it – get the dirty water off ya chests!'

It's raining outside, the grass is cool and soft, the black soil slippery mud between my toes and John does not want to fight.

I hit him on the nose, and again in the mouth, and again, and again, and when I stop – panting – he just stands there bleeding. Not once did he try and hit me.

Heads at the open windows pull back.

The rain is heavier now and it washes some of the blood from John's face – he uses a wet towel for the rest – it is mostly his nose and a swelling lip. He doesn't speak.

I make another set of boards – but the rain becomes a torrent. There will be no further crutching for at least a week, and suddenly the weekend and Inez are possible.

***

'Hello Inez – '

'Hullo Michael – '

Words are hard to catch.

We smile, we go to the beach, we swim, we lie pale on the sand – I take photos – I have them still – emotions so intense her eyes demur from the lens.

Our hands touch – by awkward accident.

We are surrounded by an intensity of parental supervision – as though we may commit something unspeakable. Looking back I realise there might have been some small social imbalance between my world and Inez's, that Inez must be kept out of reach, although it didn't strike me then.

Then it was just another hurdle.

There is a moment, Lucy and Simon are talking on the deck, I don't know where my parents are, and I find myself in the bedroom Lucy and Inez share – it is unplanned and it is minutely planned – and I lie beside Inez in her bed. And for a long time we do not even touch.

It is as if we have all the time that ever was – and we just lie there. We are both sunburnt – and we lie beside each other and slowly our thumping hearts begin to beat with the same beat – eventually my fingers touch her face at the same moment hers touch mine, and that is our first kiss.

Her lips are soft, but our teeth grate. We learn to lie still with our lips pressing softly. Her mouth opens and I taste the warmth of her tongue.

And my body hardens of its own accord – as if it lives a separate life – and it is not something I had sought, this abrupt intrusion.

'What's that?' And Inez laughs, but she presses heavy against me and my hands touch her and she touches me and what has been an intrusion becomes something else and there is never any if there is only how and we strive towards each other, shyly at first and then shy no longer and somehow we cross that rickety bridge together – a bridge to a place where mysteries become clear, where gods might have lived.

It is a simple matter then to subvert the constraints that surround us. Simon I do not think is entirely aware, but Lucy – Lucy is complicit. Lucy and Simon like each other in a friendly sort of a way – I think she would like it to be deeper, but she seems willing to settle for whatever is offered.

And Lucy makes it quite clear – in ways so obvious they attract no attention – when they will be away and when they will return.

Inez and I are consumed by each other.

'Oh we just went for a walk along the beach – don't worry Mum, we've got torches.'

'I think she's sleeping, she got a touch of the sun today.'

'Oh the poor dear – perhaps I should take her some calamine lotion for the tender spots?'

'No – Mrs Stevens – I think just let her sleep.'

'Michael must have got burnt too – he's gone to bed.'

'I'm feeling a bit sick Mrs Stevens – I don't think I'll go on the boat.'

'You poor darling, Inez – perhaps we shouldn't go.'

'Don't worry Mum – I'll stay here – she'll be okay.'

'That's very sweet of you Michael. It's such a lovely day and Simon and Lucy are so looking forward to the boat, to say nothing of your father. Would you like a glass of Ovaltine dear?'

And in that wantonly empty house unthinkable liberties blossom.

Inez

***

The weekend is over.

That the weekend would end both of us acknowledged in some distant, unvisited portion of our minds – but the reality is crushing, murderous.

Neither of us can speak.

'High time you two boys got back to work.'

University looms closer, with all its infinite promise, and Simon and I are increasingly subjected to those things which will be good for us, as if sheep will somehow anchor us to reality.

This time it is the dipping of old ewes for lice – three weeks off shears so their cuts have healed and the arsenic won't poison them. It's a plunge dip – a concrete slot too narrow for them to turn, filled with arsenic liquid. Once in they must swim to the other end before they stagger up the steps. While they swim we push them under with maple-shafted dipsticks.

We start at first light with the old ewes, they run better at first light, but soon the dip-smell drifts back from the draining pens, a thousand waiting sheep catch the smell, remember it, dig their hard little toes in and refuse to move.

We shout at them, we jump, we wave our arms, flap tatters of jute, rattle old tin lids on loops of number eight fencing wire, but the sheep wedge themselves in the back corners, pack against the back rails.

Bend over the rail – grab them by ear and greasy arse and drag them one by struggling one up the race into the dip.

Dust thickens, tempers thin, and the sun climbs above

the trees.

My father has a rule – no dogs in the yards – but Dad is up at the house and Rusty has followed me down to the shearing shed, yapping outside the yards. He isn't a big dog, Rusty. He isn't even a sheep dog. He's just a little Australian Terrier with a yapping bark, getting a bit grey around the muzzle.

I put him down beside the race. He yaps, the sheep surge up the race.

'That's what the old bitches need' grins Bob.

Rusty runs up and down the outside of the race, yapping at the sheep.

Five hundred more old ewes have been dipped, powdered sheep-shit gilds the air, and a quietness falls on the yards.

Bob nudges me – 'The Boss is here.'

I look up.

Dad's black horse is tied up under an apple tree and Dad is climbing awkwardly over the yards, his face already frozen in a look that ices my stomach.

Rusty yaps at the sheep.

'Get that damn dog out of the yards!' – his face white, one of the few times I hear him swear.

The men look down, hiding grins, my own fury froths, gives me strength.

'He's doing a good job Dad – why don't you go home and let us finish?!'

For a moment it seems even the sheep hold their breath.

Dad strides forward. 'I won't have dogs in the yard!'

He grabs Rusty – perhaps he grabs him a bit quick or a bit tight – and Rusty bites him.

Dad grunts, drops the dog, sucks his bleeding hand.

'Take that dog home! Come and see me later Michael!'

My father climbs on his horse – it is only then that my smile surfaces.

***

There is a pencilled letter addressed to me in that big round hand I recognise instantly.

'Don't write any more letters to Inez – you can send them to me if you must. Lucy.'

Inez is not well. That's all I can find out. She's been taken home from school – Lucy will tell me no more.

A door has slammed shut in some seamless globe that encloses Inez – a globe from which I am forever excluded.

It is three years before I see her again.

When we do meet it is in a rustle of dead yesterdays, our words as meaningless as autumn leaves.

NULLARBOR

Drake Abrams woke, turned on the bedside lamp, checked his watch. 4 am.

It hadn't always been Abrams – back on the other side of the world it had a bobble of syllables to tangle your tongue in – ending in 'ski'.

But he liked the sound of 'Doctor Abrams will see you now' from his new receptionist. To be truthful Drake had been shortened a bit too, but it fitted nicely now.

Beside him in the bed his wife Lorna stirred. Lorna of the soft lips and compliant nature. Compliant rated high on his list of desirable attributes in a woman. His new receptionist was compliant.

Drake stretched, kicked off the doona, got up and did some knee bends, toe touches and sit ups beside the bed – with purposeful grunting. Then he dropped his blue silk pyjamas on the floor, put on sneakers, tracksuit and beanie and walked out the door closing it loudly.

Lorna gave a small sigh and pulled the pillow over her head. She had another two hours while he walked to the paper shop, bought The Australian and The Financial Review and settled down to read them over a double shot cappuccino at Ziggi's.

Lorna pulled the pillow tighter about her head. Sometimes she got back to sleep – sometimes not. For all his early morning noises Drake was not a fit man – not flabby exactly, but with a certain mid-European softness to him. Middle aged she supposed, with a bit of a bulge over the top of his underpants that he patted from time to time in a remonstrative sort of a way.

Not that she was about to say anything – definitely not. The new receptionist was definitely attractive. Moira – even the name was a bit like hers.

Lorna had been Drake's receptionist in the early days, before the money started to build up. Who'd have thought it? – Cosmetic surgery of all things.

Drake had adopted the early morning regime two weeks ago. They had been asked on a trip across the Nullarbor – the great treeless plain across the bottom of Australia.

'It is camping trip in 4-wheel-drive Mercedes's – two of them for eight of us and a third one with all the tents, the food, the help.'

'Camping? I didn't know you liked camping dear.'

'They do it all for you, pitch tents, cook meals, serve wine – I said yes. You will enjoy.'

And Lorna supposed she would. She tried to enjoy Drake's plans – it was better that way. And besides, going for a walk to buy the paper and coffee was better than turning on the news at four o'clock in the morning. The set was too close to the bed to hide from, even under the pillows.

Drake regarded the invitation as something of a social endorsement. The other three couples did a lot of things together – had done for years – friends from schooldays some of them, although there was one English couple. And the women did daunting things for charities – Lorna wondered how she would fit in. She'd never been camping, didn't particularly like animals, not even dogs. And especially not ants.

Still, she supposed that sort of thing would be taken care of. It should be – at over a thousand dollars a day – each. Fifteen days, thirty something thousand dollars. She still couldn't get used to the money.

Well, it was Drake's idea, and his money. At least they'd be out of reach of the new receptionist.

'Read that,' Drake said at breakfast, throwing down the newspaper open at an article about a fossilised marsupial lion. *Thylacoleo carnifex.*

'Why on earth would I want to read that?'

'Because it is being discovered fifty metres down in a limestone cave under the Nullarbor. The Nullarbor is a limestone plateau, lot of caves and sinkholes. Animals fall down them – plenty other skeletons in this cave too.'

'Yes, well, I don't suppose a fifty metre fall would do anything much good. Other than a bat. I certainly wouldn't enjoy it.'

'Read it Lorna, you will find it interesting.'

And she did – she learnt about the Naracoorte caves and half a million years of animals trapped in pit-falls, now fossils, at the eastern end of the limestone formations, just west of the Victorian border.

And so many other caves, right across the Nullarbor to far Western Australia. Where they'd made this latest find, the first complete skeleton of *Thylacoleo carnifex.* The marsupial lion. Of course they weren't saying exactly where they'd found it.

It sounded quite dangerous, all those animals falling into all those caves.

***

Jim Mitchell met their plane at Alice Springs Airport rugged up like an Eskimo.

'Real brass monkey weather out here right now – minus seven out beyond the Olgas last night.'

Lorna hadn't thought it would be that cold. Nobody had said anything.

'Perhaps we should buy jackets and things here while we can,' she said to Drake.

'Do not fuss' said Drake.

The truck was battered white – smeared in red dust, two large cracks wriggling their way across the windscreen.

On the back was part of some digging machinery, a worn tooth polished silver smooth from biting into the earth's crust. A cobweb of ropes held the heavy lump to the tray of the truck.

A dog hung its head through the bars behind the cab – white hair scratched twenty four hours on end for a year or so. Lorna looked at the dog as she walked past, an ear twitched, sad eyes followed her.

A man sat in the truck, one lean brown elbow out the window – dark blue singlet, bristled beard, squinted eyes. Drake wore calf length shorts, yellow suede boots – Columbia shirt with all the pockets, wide leather hat. The man waited until Drake had reached the first of the Mercedes, and then he turned his head, spat into the red dust.

Sally Morgan, wife of Sir Jeffrey Morgan, English heart surgeon, introduced them to Jim Mitchell.

'Jim darling, we'd like you to meet Drake Abrams and the

lovely Lorna. Drake is doing wonderful things for people who want to stay young – and can afford to. They say his patients read like Who's Who.' Sally laughed.

'Except that he won't tell us who.'

She laughed again.

Jim shook Lorna's hand. There really was a rugged outdoors look about him, and he had the nicest eyes. Lorna found herself smiling into them – luckily Drake was looking over the Mercedes wagons.

'Pneumatic suspension eh? Beat the shit out of springs – I bet you.'

Jim Mitchell smiled, nodded.

***

Drake awoke with the certainty that his stomach was no longer able to contain the things he had loaded into it last night.

Dinner on this their third night into the journey had been a long loud affair, with a serious attack mounted on the considerable wine cellar in what had become known as the Chuck Wagon.

'Do you think you ought to drink all that red wine Drake? After the curry? Remember what happened last time you ate curry?

'Do not be such a pathetic wetting blanket Lorna – why you not piss off to bed, huh?'

Drake's grammar tended to slip a bit sometimes. Lorna rose.

'I think I might leave you boys to it' said Sally Morgan.

'Me too' said Frances getting up from the fire.

'Now look what you have done' said Drake.

That day they had covered some four hundred kilometres South-west into the edge of the Nullarbor.

Frances Windsor, wife of Paul Windsor, stockbroker, had them in fits at breakfast telling how she'd taken her little trowel out in the dark the night before and the huge white headlight of a train – a train for god's sake – had come thundering across the plains catching her with her pants down.

Lorna could never tell something like that.

Jim said 'A pilot told me the Nullarbor horizon is so unencumbered that flying over it you can actually see the curvature of the earth.'

'Surely you can see that curvature over oceans?' said Sir Jeffrey. Lorna still thought of him as Sir Jeffrey, although she managed to call him Jeffrey. And of course she never thought of Sally as Lady Morgan. Drake had Sir Jeffreyed and Lady Morganned them to pieces that first night, until Sally had said "Oh for god's sake Drake – "

'Guess so' said Jim. 'That's just what some pilot told me.'

'I think you can see curvatures from the train.' Mark Cowan, lawyer. Louise, his wife, bones of a sparrow, ate only fruit and yoghurt, drank only water, made Lorna feel guilty.

The others laughed – Lorna smiled.

'It'll be cold tonight' said Jim Mitchell. 'Make sure you use the cold-weather sleeping bags.'

The tents were very comfortable – thick soft floors, double roofed and double walled – sleeping bags on light foam mattresses, battery neon lamps. And the little trowels. There was a shower tent, with a gas hot water thing that lit up when you turned the tap. Only one minute each under the shower though. Lorna was surprised how much you could get done in one minute.

Drake turned on the tent lamp, looked at his watch. Two-thirty a.m.

His stomach gave a gurgle of borborygmi, and he was seized with a bowel cramp of such compelling force that he scrambled from his sleeping bag, undid the tent flies and ran barefoot into the night clad only in silk pyjamas. No time for the trowel, not even a torch.

Drake could see nothing in the velvet blackness of the night – the remorseless urgency of his bowels drove him – he must get some distance from the camp while he still could, lest the impending gastric explosion be heard – heard and laughed at. Besides which it would stink.

Lorna rolled over and switched off the lamp.

Drake ran into the night, the ground so cold his feet felt as if they were pressing on hot coals. The pain distracted him momentarily from the convulsions of his bowels. The frosted ground crunched under his bare feet. It was amazing there was enough moisture in the air to freeze.

Gott it was cold.

He ran blindly forward into the dark. The running added warmth, but it also agitated his bowels until at last he must stop, pull down his silk pyjamas and succumb to the turmoil within.

A foetid splattering discharge fuelled by curry and red wine scalded sensitive flesh – soaked his silk pyjama pants – at least it was hot.

Until finally his intestines contracted and expelled the last scalding drizzle and the night air chilled and then froze whatever had reached naked skin.

Still crouching Drake edged his feet out of his pyjama pants – by feel he folded the wet patches inside and wiped himself clean as best he could in the dark.

That was the end of the pyjamas. He scratched a shallow hole in the frosted crust, buried them, covered them, stood up. The dark reeled about him until he thought he might fall, but gradually he steadied.

He looked around.

Nothing.

Overhead stars sparkled diamond clear – but there was no moon. Stars did not cast much light – in spite of what poets might say – certainly not enough to find his way.

And he had absolutely no idea of whatever it was sailors might extract from the stars to guide them on their travels.

Just a bunch of meaningless pinpricks in the thick black blanket of the night.

Drake turned slowly in a circle, scanning the horizon – and there it was – a light. Probably the one he had left on in the tent.

Gruss Gott. It was freezing out here barefoot in silk pyjama shirt.

He would have shower in the shower tent. He had used his minute already this night, but he was so cold. Just the thought of that flaring gas ring and its steaming water warmed him.

And he stank.

Drake started running towards the light. If only he had a torch.

Something needle-like pierced his foot – he stopped – brushed the sole of his foot with fingers so clumsy with cold they could hardly feel – broke off a spiky thorn, one of those four-pronged needles that grew on cacti. The soles of his feet burnt with the cold. His arms, his legs, his whole body trembled with shivering cold. Shivering was good, it was the muscles contracting to warm themselves. He must keep running, never mind the prickles.

He ran on towards the distant light – it was more of a hobble than a run now – cramp clutching his left calf – searing fingers reaching up to seize the back of his left thigh. His body had expelled too much fluids. Allergic reaction to the curry? His throat felt tight, his breath wheezed. Was he entering anaphylactic shock? And at that thought his bowels convulsed again and he must stop. The contractions now felt dangerous.

How long since last time? Twenty minutes?

The light was no closer. It even seemed a little higher – but that was not possible.

Unless it was a star.

He tried to rise from his squat but his left leg would not lift. The world inside his head tilted sharply, slid down a long slope. His right leg pushed until he tipped over, face down in rank warmth. His leg spasmed stiff. He sucked at air through a throat rapidly closing.

***

Lorna woke to an empty tent, the sun drawing sparkles from

the white mantle of frost outside the open tent flap. Drake must have come back and gone out again early – without waking her for once. He had been up early every morning of this camping trip – not once zipping the tent flaps shut so she could snuggle down in the fug of her sleeping bag.

None of the others got up so early – except Paul Winsor, the stockbroker. He was always pissing somewhere – (she could say words like that to herself) – when they'd shared a vehicle with the Windsors they had to stop practically every hour. Prostate like as not Drake said.

She sometimes heard Paul in the night – he didn't bother with a trowel – occasionally she got a waft. More lethal than breast cancer Drake said.

Poor man thought Lorna.

Breakfast started at eight-thirty – the smell of crisping bacon and fresh brewed coffee drew Lorna to the breakfast table. Fresh fruit and yoghurt, eggs with bacon and maple syrup – it should be illegal thought Lorna, but god she loved it.

So did Drake – he was always first to the breakfast table.

Not today.

'Where's Drake?' asked Jim.

Lorna shook her head. 'Must be still walking – you know what he's like.'

Jim grinned at her – a grin that warmed her more than the winter sun. 'Bacon and eggs? The usual?'

Lorna smiled, nodded. 'Yes please Jim, tomatoes, hash browns, maple syrup, toast, marmalade – the lot – I feel so sinful.'

'It suits you Lorna – talk about morning glory' and Jim actually blushed under his tan, blushed and turned away like a small boy.

She put a hand on his forearm. He looked at her then. Those eyes.

'Here come the others – morning Jeffrey, Sally, Mark, Louise. Hi Frances – Paul coming?'

Frances Windsor nodded. 'He had a restless night – the curry he says – of course it wasn't the wine. Oh no.

'He can't drink wine. Whiskey's okay, but not wine – and Paul loves his wine.

'Where's Drake?'

'Still walking I guess' said Lorna.

'Not like Drake to be late for breakfast' said Sir Jeffrey.

***

'I'm getting a bit concerned about Drake' said Jim. 'It's half past nine now – we'll have to pack up pretty soon.'

Lorna was beginning to wonder too. She'd had a good look out across the plain after breakfast – no-one was walking in towards the camp, and you could see for miles. Just the odd clump of Saltbush, right to the edge of the world.

The sparkle of frost had gone, but the air was still cold, the Westerly already brushing feathers of dust off the ground.

Jim climbed the little ladder to the top of the Chuck Wagon – carefully scanned all the way around the horizon with a pair of binoculars.

He jumped down, shook his head at Lorna's questioning look.

'Nothing. Think I'll take one of the vehicles and have a look. Want to come?'

Lorna nodded. 'He might have twisted an ankle or something.'

They returned to the camp at half past eleven. 'Hasn't turned up while we've been away?'

Mark Cowan, looking very serious, shook his head. 'Shouldn't we be calling someone?' Louise nodded. 'Yes Jim – don't you think you ought to call a search helicopter or something?'

Jim Mitchell climbed up on the Chuck Wagon again with his binoculars.

Lorna saw him pause part way through his scan. She looked where he had stopped. Was that black speck high in the dark blue sky an eagle? Jim got down, looked at her questioningly and she climbed into the wagon with him. Jim drove towards the distant speck.

***

Three big eagles flapped up on heavy wings – one of them seemed to have its talons tangled in something, but it lifted free eventually.

A dozen shiny black crows hopped then flew a little distance, landed on the desert, watching.

A fox trotted away reluctantly towards a clump of Saltbush, looking back.

Lorna was surprised by how quickly they had done their

work.

Looking at what remained below the blue silk pyjama shirt – she suddenly thought of Moira the new receptionist. The thought brought a smile to her lips – a smile she quickly covered with her hand.

'You okay?' asked Jim softly, putting an arm around her.

Lorna allowed herself to be drawn against him, nodding into his chest.

GOLDEN FIELDS FOREVER

She sat on the low stone wall, ruffled sea below, her long hair caught in the wind's fingers, the lonely cry of seagulls speaking in the voice of her heart.

He was the only man she had ever drawn to her – the only man who had ever asked her for more than another drink – give us three schooners of VB darl, and one of New – they spoke to her hands, never her eyes, and she took their crumpled notes and their wet coins, slid their change across the bar and turned to the next blurred face.

But Tom was different.

Tom had seen her face, her eyes, he had looked right at her and she had seen the tremor in his look as he caught her inward eye – before his gaze moved to her other, more predictable combination of sclera, iris and pupil.

He had smiled at her, smiled at her good eye – a vestige of that smile had slipped cautiously to her left eye, hesitated, and then drifted back, unhurriedly, to her more reliable optic.

That small slow second drift of his eyes warmed her heart. She smiled a small smile, her lips large with the unaccustomed exercise.

And Tom had smiled back.

Of course she didn't know he was Tom then, but he was someone, someone more than a mouth and hands and she drew herself up a little behind the bar – lifted her shoulders and eased her not inconsiderable breasts out of their habitual slump.

His eyes slid downward at the movement and her body tingled beneath his gaze. She stood straight, pink wool tightening – and this time when he looked up she had a smile ready to meet his.

Her smile widened, her body taking on a shape that was almost naughty – and for the first time she let it.

She tossed her head and her heavy mane of hair whipped out in a dark column, her breasts shook in outlandish fashion beneath the pink wool – well it would have been outlandish – except that her heavy bra caught the exuberant flesh before it could become indecent and scrunched it down into a sort of squashed tremor.

But the thought was there.

'What time d'you get off, sweetheart?' he had asked and 'ten-thirty' she had said without a moment's thought – or regret.

And Tom had been waiting outside the door as the sign flickered off in the night.

'Feel like a walk darlin?'

And she had nodded, taken his hand and they had strolled down the pavement past the darkened shops to the green grass beneath the Norfolk pines and the crush of small waves folding on the beach.

They had sat together on the wooden bench overlooking the bay and she had been in no doubt at all about what was going to happen.

'My name's Tom darlin, what's yours?' and she had said

'Pauline.'

'Pauline, that's a nice name. Been working at the Green Hat long?'

'Six months.'

'Six months eh? Didn't realise I'd been away so long' and his arm had slipped across her shoulders, his hand falling comfortably on her breast and she had raised herself towards it.

'Lovely tits darlin' he had said and his other hand had held her and he had kissed her and she had kissed him back and they had found a small hollow in the short grass and the quiet surge of the waves had slowly receded beneath the heavy pulse of her own blood in her ears.

And they had slept.

The clock was loud in her empty room.

She had a small photo of her mother in a red dress, the same dark hair, dark eyes, the picture sitting on the small chest of drawers beside the mirror.

She had no photo of her father – the only one she had ever seen was the one of her mother and a group of sailors, some holding bottles, the same red dress – her father was the second on the left her mother said.

When the Welfare found her and told her of her mother's death the small box of possessions they had given her held no picture of sailors.

There were old letters in the bottom of the box – letters from people she did not know. There was one that said

Dear Mavis our ship docks at Woolloomooloo Saturday

week, meet you at Harry's café de wheels eight-thirty Saturday night. Jim.

Was Jim second from the left? Or were there other Jims?

Pauline took the box from the bottom drawer which it shared with her black vinyl handbag and a second sweater – green this one – and searched the old writing paper for truths it would not reveal.

She lay on her lumpy bed, the murmur of distant waves finding their way in through the open window, and let her mind drift back to memories of her mother.

'Don't talk about sex in front of the cat' Mavis had cautioned with a tilt of her head towards Pauline, and Mavis's friend – it was Hilda – had smiled and sipped her rum and coke. It had been in a bar in a hotel, another bar, another hotel, they had been her second, her third, her twenty-fifth homes. There had been no place where she had been able to gather toys and pets the way other children could.

She had a cat once – a small tabby thing that she had found in the street, and she had taken it to their room and fed it milk from the small carton in the rattling fridge in the corridor and it had slept on her bed. And one day coming back from whatever school she had been attending she had found it squashed in the street outside the boarding house they then called home.

That had been her only pet.

After her mother's funeral she had taken jobs in hotels, first as a cleaner, later as a barmaid, and she had found The Green Hat six months ago. She liked living beside the ocean – her room wasn't much – it was noisy on Saturday nights but she was usually working then anyway – and it came free with the job.

She supposed it was free because no paying guest would ever take it – just a narrow slot at the end of the hall beside the broom cupboard with one small window facing the street.

Pauline lay on the bed and gazed at the light on the wall from the street-light –remembering Tom.

He had been nice. Not hurried, not rough – he had taken his time and had somehow managed to lead them both to where they wanted to go, and Pauline had heard enough gossip in enough hotel kitchens to know that wasn't always the way things were.

Especially if you happened to have an eye like hers.

She hadn't felt him leave her side. She just woke and he wasn't there.

Six months later and Mrs Johnston the hotel Manageress came up to her closing time Saturday night.

'Finish up now Pauline – I'll need your room tomorrow – got a new girl coming Monday.'

Just like that.

Pauline hadn't realized she was showing so clearly – she had worn loose clothes the last couple of months, but Mrs Johnston didn't miss much. It'd be hard to get another job now – she had a little bit of money saved, two hundred and seventy five dollars – it would have to last her three months – she could look no further than that.

She had one bag, a squashy nylon thing, dark blue with handles and a zip. It held all her possessions quite easily, including her mother's cardboard box. She sat on the bed Sunday morning looking at the bag, wondering where she would go in an untroubled sort of way. It didn't make much difference.

She might be able to get a kitchen job somewhere – or a cleaner's job – some of those contract cleaners took you on without too much fuss. The work was hard though – she'd only be able to do it for a few weeks even if she found a spot.

Mrs Johnston nodded briefly when she handed in her key at the desk. She walked out the front door and wandered down the road towards the bus stop. There was no point in staying here. And she didn't want to go back to the Welfare.

The Welfare stuck their noses into every corner of your life – they pried and poked among the cobwebs and came up with all the little things that didn't really count anywhere – except with them.

Like who's your father for instance.

And when they asked that question they used a different voice – and the voice said quite clearly in its own way that if you didn't know who your father was you were definitely at fault. We know all about people like you. We don't use words like illegitimate or bastard. Dear me no.

We use nice words like unknown.

But those words are still there, nudging, winking furtively, hiding in a frown or widened eyes or the twitch of a lip.

The blue bag nudged Pauline's leg as she walked down to the bus stop. The sun was bright, seagulls sat clean and white on the stone wall and small waves rustled on the beach. For no good reason she crossed the road and the small expanse of grass and settled on the wall beside the seagulls, beneath the sighing Norfolk pines.

Three pelicans stood beside the water, wings agape.

Behind her a bus squeaked slowly to a stop, doors whooshed. A rumble of engine, an ascending whine of gears and it faded into the distance.

Seagulls fluttered up off the wall beside her and a figure sat down.

The pelicans did not move.

Pauline heard the chime of steel halyards against metal masts of moored boats bobbing in the bay.

GLOBAL SEAWEED

Sally was bored shitless at Bio Invest Global. She didn't give a flying fuck if she never saw another *Jatropha* plant – if she never heard the name *Jatropha* again.

Sally was attractive in a dark and vulnerable way – High Distinctions in Statistical Analyses and Experimental Design, no more than a dancing acquaintance with Botany in general – like she'd done Botany II, she knew the green stuff – but maths was her field.

B.I.G. had made her an offer practically as soon as the results came out and she'd jumped at it – that was where the smart boys went. But nobody told her the entire staff walked around the place like they had pokers up their arses and only spoke to the Prof. or themselves.

The Prof. ran the show – sixty if he was a day, swam a kilometre every morning and slid his hands up the skirts of whatever secretary was in his office at eleven a.m. And he was smart – smarter than all the rest of them put together Sally reckoned. When he looked at her with what Sally thought of as that Anthony Hopkins look – the one Hopkins reserved for Jodie Foster, without the mask – well anyway when he looked at her like that she felt about ten years old – and with the feeling that part of her underwear was missing.

So far she'd managed to avoid his office mid-morning.

The one bright note in the whole equation was David Seaborne – hair the colour of bleached straw, eyes blue as a summer sky and shoulders wide as a wool bale. David was a hunk and Sally had a weakness for hunks – and he was totally unaware of his hunkhood, if there was such a word.

It gave her momentary pause actually – she'd brushed against him enough times at the old morning tea table to get the message across – but no lights had lit.

Well he'd smiled at her of course – he'd smiled at her but there hadn't been any kicker juice – no hint of the hot squidgy stuff.

So she'd talked to him about his Jatropha.

And that was when something happened in those eyes – up until then if she was being honest they'd been as empty as the skies they reminded her of – not even the odd parrot of lust flicking across the vacant space.

Anyway Jatropha did the trick – not that it was much of a trick – everybody in this research lab a thousand miles from the back of nowhere – well one of those side streets running off the highway out at Liverpool if you wanted to be picky – everyone in the whole unlovely aircraft hangar of a building talked about Jatropha.

Seeds of the Jatropha plant held oil that could run a diesel engine. That was the guts of it.

'We're making the plant tolerant to glyphosate,' he said to Sally. 'That's my project.'

'You mean like Roundup Ready?' Well she had to say something, and that sounded about right. It was more than enough.

'Yes!' said David. 'Yes, we took we took a glyphosate tolerant gene from Agrobacterium, cloned it, used a petunia plasmid to inject it into Jatropha by particle acceleration along with a marker gene encoding beta-glucaronidase – we call that GUS.' He smiled at such a charming little idiosyncrasy.

Sally winced.

'GUS turns an indicator substrate blue, where you've got GUS you've got glyphosate tolerance – we hope.'

David smiled, and there was zing in the smile for the first time. Maybe if she wore a little sprig of Jatropha in her hair?

'Anyway – now we're testing the resultant strains for glyphosate tolerance.'

'Is it working?'

'Yes – I'll say, working like a charm.'

He looked so appealing Sally reached out and touched his forearm with it's down of golden hair.

'Why don't you come around to my place tonight – I'll make dinner and you can tell me all about it?'

'Oh gee – thanks Sally – I'd really like that. You sure it's no trouble?'

'No – no trouble David – I'd really like to hear about it.' Holy shit – well she could always turn the stereo up, or wear ear plugs.

***

Sally learnt a lot more about Jatropha than she really needed. Over dinner *Jatropha curacas* emerged as the frontrunner, maybe the only runner in David's world.

Sally had plunged for oysters mornay – well why not – she loved them. Not those tasteless things quick frozen in cheese flavoured Plaster of Paris.

For Sally it was Sydney Rock oysters – fresh from the sea that morning, still weeping hot salty tears under a crust of cheese simmering with golden flakes and crumbling pinnacles of pleasure.

When she lifted those juicy dripping moments of ecstasy to her lips and bit down on the hot flesh paroxysms of the Pacific filled her mouth – oral orgasms of oceans. So to speak.

She watched David dig into the first cheese encrusted shell.

'Gee Sally, these are nice oysters. You've done something to them.'

Sally had served Bloody Marys beforehand – one small can of tomato juice and half a bottle of vodka – just as well she'd been generous with the Worcestershire source. Even though David had drunk two thirds of the jug, she was feeling a little numb by the champagne. She was hoping David might bring something; it turned out to be a box of muesli bars.

There was fish, then chocolate mousse with a shitload of rum and a coulis of crushed strawberries and she opened her last bottle of Botrytis Semillon. David drank two thirds of the champagne without apparently noticing, which was just as well because Sally found the table had developed a pronounced tilt. Nothing alarming, but there.

Sally managed to get him on the sofa for coffee – it was a small sofa and she only served one cup each – and by the time the last of the botrytis had disappeared things had taken a turn for the better.

Sally was wearing very little under what she wasn't wearing much of, and after a while David couldn't help noticing. From then on things moved along quite nicely – it might not have quite matched the moments engendered by the oysters – but Sally put that down to a bit much botrytis.

But it was nice to look across the rumpled bed at that golden arrangement of arms and legs and all the rest of it – all blond, too. Sally liked that.

She reached out a hand across that vast expanse of chest, tweaked a nipple, started sliding south.

'Do you know the West Australian Government has banned the cultivation of *Jatropha gossypifolia*?'

Sally's hand stopped like it had been severed at the shoulder.

'No shit?"

'Yes! Can you believe it?'

This was pillow talk? Out of nowhere an ancient movie of that name – Rock Hudson and Doris Day in bed – one critic had said "sexy as two Cadillacs parked side by side." Rock had been gay hadn't he? Somebody trying to tell her something here?

'What's *Jatropha gossypifolia*?'

'Well – it's actually called Bellyache Bush.'

'Bellyache Bush! I love that! What is it – poisonous or something?'

'Yeah – well it is actually – but banning it! I mean it could be an important source of biodiesel.'

'Is it?'

'We don't know yet – but they've banned it – I mean how stupid can you get?'

'Is it poisonous to people and animals, or just people?'

'Well both actually – but that's hardly the point.'

Sally chose her next words with care. Make it clean she told herself.

'Yes well – I'm with them. Poisonous to everyone and everything? – ban it – hell yes.'

***

Sally was summoned to the Prof's office – she checked her watch – 11 am on the dot. She wondered about the lab coat, hung it on its peg, walked down the corridor in her miniskirt, knocked on the door, entered his office.

The Prof rose from behind his desk.

'Sally dear, how nice to see you – have a seat.'

Sally lowered herself into a deep armchair, by the time she came to rest her bottom was considerably lower than her knees. The Prof took a chair opposite. Sally decided this was quite fun – well more fun than David Seaborne. Sally crossed her legs.

'Care to help yourself to coffee dear?' and the Prof nodded at a little table in the corner. Sally climbed out of the armchair, poured herself a cup of coffee, returned to her chair and sank into its depths without spilling a drop. She reckoned the Prof was getting his money's worth.

'Sally dear – how would you like to go to Fiji?'

'Fiji? – and leave all this?' waving her arms at the grey building that surrounded them.

The Prof smiled, and Sally wondered what it was going to

cost. Funny thing was she didn't see it as a cost at all. She was glad of the miniskirt.

'Fiji sounds just gorgeous Chris. But why Fiji?'

Chris for christ's sake – she'd never called him anything but Professor Lawson until now – but well – Fiji? – definitely Chris.

'We're setting up a research station outside Savu Savu.' Sally nodded wisely but she didn't have a clue where Savu Savu was.

'It's a little town on the northern island of Vanua Levu – a bit off the beaten tourist track, but we're very conscious of biosecurity, so we need somewhere out of the way.'

Liverpool by the sea? Sally wondered.

'Our research station is in a bay that shelters behind a coral reef – coconut palms, breadfruit, banana trees, tropical jungle.'

Probably not Liverpool by the sea.

'Our research in Fiji is focused on marine algae in tropical environments. We're looking to develop a high carbohydrate algae that we can ferment to yield around 2000 litres of ethanol per hectare three of four times a year.'

'Wow – that sounds a lot,' said Sally.

'If we're successful there are contractors ready to grow it under licence in the bay – our early target would be around 1000 hectares.'

Sally did a quick little calculation – at a dollar a litre that came in at around $16,000,000 a year.

***

Sally was billeted in a little resort outside of Savu Savu. From the deck of her bure she watched coconut palms scratch the sky, the crowns armoured with clustered hand grenades. And they were so tall! One of those coconuts hit you on its way to earth – . Sally hadn't actually seen one fall so far, but early mornings there were a few half-buried in the soft lawns – harvested each day by the Fijian staff.

The mottled beetroot leaves of ginger plants burst up outside the bure, breadfruit trees with leaves like hands, serrated trunks and clusters of green breadfruit, frangipanni, bushes of flowers in pink lipped cascades, and one secretive little palm that hid flowers like red and yellow tropical birds unwinding down twisting stems.

Banana palms, Raintrees, trees she'd never heard of, the lawn pocked with burrows of unseen landcrabs. Toads hopped wetly at night, birds sang unstoppable music in early mornings, a determined rooster tried to drag the sun up at three a.m. and fruit bats flapped their leathery ways about the tops of the palms on dusk. Sally even found a curious mongoose on her doorstep.

And the rain. Sometimes warm and light, sometimes warm and heavy, sometimes warm and so deafening on the iron roofs that conversation just died, and she might drown just taking her next breath. Such rain was too much for the few gutters and downpipes.

And then the rain stopped, gutters trickled, grass sogged, the rain drained away, soaked into the rich red soil from which the jungle sprang with such indecent haste.

Plants grew a foot a day, trees carrying a load of vines and creepers that erupted into pale blue or white or yellow flowers the moment the sun appeared.

When the sun did appear Sally heard the jungle creaking with the surge of new growth. The air was soft, warm, fecund, the water soft and warm as the air.

Sally had always thought of soft water only as water fit to drink, but now she knew salt water could be soft. Now she knew that hard water was water that held memories of ice.

This water that caressed arms and legs and fishes with warm intimacy – this water that allowed fabulous creatures to blossom in outrageous colour, this water that nurtured convoluted rainbowed imaginings of coral in its sunny shallows – this water was truly soft.

Soft as the wave of a mermaid's tail.

***

Sam Lepstein was overseas – Sam was the coordinator of the project. Sally walked out to the research centre, the shed of concrete and corrugated iron on the foreshores of a mangrove-filled inlet beyond the town – the shed an array of concrete ponds and tubs and elevated glass tanks and a couple of technicians who supervised the gurgling water in the tanks.

The whole place was double netted with stainless steel gauze under a long iron roof.

There was nothing for Sally to do and she did it beautifully. She allowed the somnolence of the island to surround her. She no longer woke each morning to the desperate rooster or even the trilling birds. Not even the slow pulsing throb of the combination cargo ship and passenger liner pulling out of Savu Savu at daylight, after trundling in on dark, lights ablaze.

And then Sam Lepstein returned. Sam was tall, dark, bearded from ear to ear, and fat. Fat face, thick beard a furry animal nesting around his neck, fat eyelids, fat forehead and a belly that was vast, tented in a dark shirt, the shirt ending in a pair of shorts that clung to the extreme perimeter of that belly in defiance of all the laws of physics.

Sam had a booming voice and a wife, Rachel, of similar if lesser physique – with the addition of long hair and long teeth. Rachel's teeth were so long and outward curving that Sally found herself thinking of horses. Rachel spent much of her time with lips parted, and for a while Sally thought she was about to say something – but this proved not to be the case.

Accompanying Sam and Rachel was Alec Stoner, and Sally's whole world changed when she saw him.

Right from the start there was something about Alec that spelt trouble – adonis body – there was no other word for it, blonde hair, lips full and wide, spreading over his whole face when he smiled, blue eyes so pale she could see coral in their shallows. And when those eyes rested on her there was no doubt about what Alec Stoner was thinking – none at all. Trouble he might be – but it would be fun. Fun and trouble was a cocktail Sally could not resist.

Sam Lepstein had not made the introductions but Alec said 'Hello – you must be Sally Farthing – what they told me didn't do you justice,' and Sally had actually felt herself blushing. This was going to be more than okay.

If there were other things in those blue eyes besides her, Sally couldn't care less – it was the message those eyes had for her that counted right at this moment – all of a sudden Sally was loaded.

Loaded with juice, the hungry heat of an inverted candle burning somewhere low inside her.

'Tell me what it is you're planning Alec, it sounds exciting.'

Even Sally thought it was a bit gushing, but shit.

'We've got a lot of marine algae specimens from the Sargasso Sea – you know the Sargasso Sea?'

'Sure – a great floating glob of seaweed somewhere in the Atlantic.'

'Right. Well, we've tried a lot of cultures of *Sargassum* genus, and the best performers are *Sargassum natans* varieties.'

Sally nodded helpfully.

'We're looking for high carbohydrate plants – and we're limited to asexual reproducers because once we establish a genotype we don't want it modified by variations from sexual reproduction.'

'Bad luck for *Sargassum natans*,' said Sally. He grinned then, and the grin alone was worth it.

'We've given the best varieties glyphosate tolerance – '

'With the GUS enzyme marker gene?' asked Sally. She never thought she'd be able to make use of that little gem, not in a million.

'That's right – ' he was looking at her like she actually knew what she was talking about. 'Not only that, but we've conferred tolerance to the new organophosphates and whatever marine pathogens we could manage. Nothing's going to kill these little suckers.'

Sally thought it sounded like a line out of Pretty Woman.

'And because all the forecasts are for increases in marine temperatures we've built that in too – at the expense of loss of low temperature tolerance, but we don't see that as a problem.'

'What happens if this stuff gets away?' Sally gave him her best wide-eyed innocent look, hoped she wasn't overdoing it. 'I mean if it gets away from the commercial contractors?'

'It won't' said Sam Lepstein. 'We've got all sorts of perimeter security systems for the contractors, and of course in the lab biosecurity is foolproof.'

'Okay – but what if it does get loose?'

'Okay – let's say it does –it'll only scrub a bit more carbon dioxide from the atmosphere – help reduce global warming. Then – because it's vegetative reproduction, not sexual reproduction, it's only an annual – it'll die out after a year, max.'

'I see – that's very clever.'

Sam Lepstein nodded.

'Going to be worth a fortune if we get it right – make a great deal of money for B.I.G.. We're patenting some of the more promising strains as we find them.'

'That's where the money is' said Alec. 'Patent the killer plants, let someone else grow them, just collect the royalties.'

'You mean it'll be the patents that are worth the money? asked Sally.

'Absolutely – keep your eye out for likely seaweeds,' said Alec, and Sally didn't think he was entirely joking.

**

There was a tap on Sally's door that night, she opened it to a smiling Alec wearing a pale green T shirt.

'Oh!' said Sally. Alec grinned at her.

'Oh' she said again, but by this time something hot and squirmy was moving in her low down, spreading quickly, even her knees seemed to be catching it. 'Oh Jesus!'

'Aren't you going to ask me in?'

'Come in.' Sally did not think she was capable of breathing any longer, let alone uttering further stupid words – and she couldn't help watch as he walked in – mesmerised like a bird with a snake and she grinned at that ludicrous pun. Oh god he had a cute little bum. Something burst inside her and oh Jesus oh Jesus oh Jesus fucking Christ and it was a tangle of legs and clothes that never seemed to get out of the way. And then it was okay oh yes it was definitely okay oh fuck me dead oh shit this is going way too quick oh fuck oh fuck oh yes quick quick yes don't stop oh holy shit –

And for a small golden sunburst of time the world stood still – utterly still and their bodies did that thing that some bodies can do and some can only dream of – until the stars fell, coalesced into pools of sweet hot honey, cooled and settled between them – settled in a world of velvet night, small sounds of restless birds and the thick scents of night-flowers.

For a long time neither of them moved – Sally could hear his soul, count the beatings of his heart.

And they slept. Except it was not sleep – no sleep was ever so sweet, so pure, so dreamless, so utter it might have been ten minutes or ten hours but Sally woke and kissed his lips and for better or worse fell in love forever.

She knew nothing of Alec – and she could not picture she could not conceive she could not imagine she did not even want to begin to think of a life that did not hold him in it.

And of course he may hold entirely different views – and

it made no difference. Her commitment, her total acceptance of him was not some transaction where they swapped mutual exclusions – she loved him and would no matter what. If there were ten other women in his life she loved him still – .

Sally knew right then that Alec was unreliable – she didn't need to be told – she knew. Knew that a time could come when he would leave her – well not leave her specifically – but just leave. And that knowledge did not dim her longing for a moment. Her passion was total, it fed on him and it grew in her and it left no choices but the slaking of it.

If this was Paradise, thought Sally, it had a thin skin.

***

Alec found the small speckled slime like tiny frogs spawn floating above a cultivar of fine hairs in one of two hundred petrii dishes.

Spores – spores in a cultivar that should only reproduce asexually.

He glanced at the label. *Sargassum natans* var. *montaigne*. Without pausing, scarcely initiating the process of thought – in a blink of certainty where all possibilities exploded Alec skimmed the slime onto a microscope slide, covered it with a fine glass cover slip, bagged it, put it in his lab-coat pocket.

He was alone at the bench with its rows of cultivars. He peered into each of the other two hundred dishes, but none had the slime of spores on their surface. The dish with the spores held a far thicker clotting of hair-like algae than any of the others.

Alec picked up the dish, poured the contents down the sink, poured half the contents of another dish into the empty dish.

Alec left the lab – walked down to the shore line – along the muddy mangrove fringe until he found it – a cup of rock reached only by King tides – that time when earth and moon and sun aligned to pull the envelope of earth's oceans into peak highs and lows.

The king tides had come five days ago – not due again for months – and the little rock pool no bigger than a spa bath was brimming with seawater, small seaweeds, crabs, periwinkles, darting speckled fish.

Alec withdrew the slide from its plastic bag, dipped it in the pond, slid the coverslip off and hoped the spores had survived. He would check later.

Alec inspected the pond the next day – nothing. Nothing the following day, nor the day after, nor the day after that. The spores must have died in his pocket. Fuck.

He'd come back in a week or so to make sure.

On the eighth day a skein of fine brown hairs spread across one corner of the pool. On the ninth day it covered half the pool, a thin scum of spawn above it.

Five seagulls flew in from the ocean, settled on the pool, darted sharp red beaks at the elusive speckled fish, plucked experimentally at the fine algal hairs – shook their heads in disgust. They preened most of the slime of spawn off their fine white feathers and flew back to the more rewarding ocean.

On the tenth day the skein of hairs had covered the pool, scummed on the rock margins – small crabs scuttled on its surface, burrowed into it. Beneath the thickening scum small speckled fish grew hungry for oxygen.

Alec reached the small pond in the dark water behind the mangroves on the twelfth day. The surface of the pond was yellowing scum with bubbles and small crabs. Alec plunged his arm through the sludge, drew up a slime of dead seaweed and one small dead fish. The algal crust had smothered life in the pond – another day and it would have smothered itself.

Alec harvested some of the fibres, some of the spores. Twelve days! Twelve days and it had taken over the entire marine community. A day later and it would have sterilised itself with the heat of its own decomposition.

***

'Sam – I want to cultivate this specimen in the lab.'

Sam shook his head. 'Sorry Alec – we've got a program that's using all our resources – there's no room for anything else.'

'Shit Sam – you can fit one more specimen in – this thing just took over a pond out there up the inlet – I found it by the sheerest chance. We've got to try it – and I want to patent it before we start.'

'Alec – it's not on. You know that.'

Sally was watching, she had no idea what they were talking about but Alec was pleading – his body was pleading – and that was enough for her. She wandered over. 'What's happening?'

'I've found this extraordinary sample of algae – collected in the inlet – it dominated a whole community and I want to cultivate it – check it out. Sam says there's no room.'

'That's what scientists are supposed to do isn't it Sam?' asked Sally. 'Observe, collect, examine, evaluate – isn't that the job of a field scientist?'

Sam nodded – reluctantly, but his fat head bobbled on his

fat neck, his brown eyes trying to hide in their folds of fat.

'And there's room in the storage shed to set up an evaluation bench isn't there?'

Sam's eyes flickered, looked down to the point of his belly where his T shirt became shorts. He nodded.

Sally shrugged – she didn't say well? – but the sound of it echoed nonetheless.

'Okay – you can set up in the storage shed Alec – do it in your own time – and if the thing's any good Bio Invest Global gets first bite at the cherry. Okay?'

'Okay man – Okay! How do I go about taking out a patent on it?'

'I can do that' said Sally. 'We've got witnesses in Sam and me that you've expressed the intention publicly – leave it with me.'

***

'It's a variation of *Sargassum natans*' said Alec. 'The boys must have washed out some of the petrii dishes there or something.'

Twenty petrii dishes stretched along the bench under the lights – each one of them clotted with hairlike algae. Sam peered closely at the dishes, half of them with blue sediment in the bottom.

'Is that a GUS reaction?'

'Yep – and I've done the glyphosate tolerance test – it's roundup ready alright – has to be an accidental contamination from the lab – but the boys will never let on.'

'That might affect your patent' said Sam. 'If it comes from our lab.'

Alec shook his head. 'It's a new variety – I've called it *Sargassum natans* var. *Lepstein.*'

'What's this?' said Sam, pointing to a small rime of scum in one of the dishes. Alec looked, shook his head.

'Looks like spooring to me' said Sam – 'give me a slide – let's mount it, have a look.'

He peered into the microscope, grunted, stood back. 'Yes – it's spores alright – this stuff is reproducing sexually – we'll have to incinerate the lot. Where did you find it?'

Alec led them all down to the rock pond, now a crusted scum of brown slime baked in the heat of its own decomposition.

'Jesus what a mess – what a stink!' said Sam. 'It doesn't look too dangerous now, we'll incinerate it just the same – thank god it didn't get away from us.'

***

'Why Alec? Why did you do it?'

He looked sharply at Sally. 'How come you're so sure it was me?'

'Oh Alec –. But why?'

'Well – those spores – I don't know, I suddenly thought I could seed it in an isolated pond, and I knew it would mutate because of the spores – and I'd have a new variety – and well – you know – I thought it would be mine. Make me rich.'

'Didn't it occur to you that your new variety might produce spores?'

Alec shrugged.

Sally smiled at that shrug, but something more demanding had come up between them.

Out in the bay a seagull floundered briefly as it shook clotted hairs from its feet. Around it was a floating brown raft big as a tennis court, crabs skittering over it, seagulls chasing them.

Beyond were other floating tennis courts, brown encrustations of algae, each one fragmenting into further floating algal mats as small waves rippled their edges, carried them out to sea with the tides.

THE WOODBOX

Lukey Pease was a scrawny piece of humanity with sallow skin, lively eyes and a foxy smile. Something about that smile let him slip under the guard of women who might no longer have a particular reason to keep their guard up.

Beth Toomey for example.

Leonard Toomey was hard and lean as the red slabs he split from the Ironbarks clinging dark and tall to the steep flanks of the ranges, his beard black and coarse as their bark. Leonard made his living leaving tangles of Ironbark crowns and stumps bleeding to death in the mountains.

He had punched two girls out of Beth – both of whom he had no patience for – and since then he had shown no interest in Beth, save at mealtimes.

Pale mornings Beth lit the cold iron Dover stove, frost wrinkled thick on the windows, taps frozen. A big soft woman Beth, she made Len hot oat porridge with brown sugar and cream, coffee in the saucepan. Half a loaf of buttered bread and a knuckle of corned beef in his lunchbag, a wedge of dark fruitcake wrapped in greaseproof paper, little cloth bags freshly filled with tea and sugar in his quartpot.

Leonard grunted when Beth set the steaming porridge bowl on the table each morning, he grunted again when she set down the dish of mutton chops and boiled potatoes and cabbage and carrots in the evening, and that was about it.

The sun was still a rumour when Leonard ground the starter in the old Ford out in the shed.

Beth was always relieved when the motor caught – Len soured down real quick if he had to crank it, and she could never work the choke and accelerator like he wanted.

The truck clattered away down the valley trailing blue smoke, and that was the last she saw of him until the sun had long died and cold dark crept up from the valley.

Lukey Pease showed up on the porch one morning out of nowhere.

'Like me to fix that screen door?'

Well she'd been after Leonard to fix it for the past year so 'Yes Lukey' she'd said, and Lukey had it back on its hinges neat as you like.

'Split a bit a wood?'

'Oh yes please,' and inside half an hour the woodbox was full of good short chunks of red ironbark just the right size for the stove door.

'Len around is he?'

'Nah – he's workin up the far side a Black Mountain – home late these days. Let me get ya a cuppa tea.'

'That sounds real nice,' and Lukey parked his bony arse on the corner of the kitchen table and chatted away to her like words were cheap.

When she'd brought him his cuppa and cake his hands had just slid down her legs and lifted her dress before she could say a word. Not that she could think of anything to say – or that she tried.

She didn't even have time to put down the tea and cake.

It had been a long time, and a lot of ground to make up, and Lukey did a pretty good job of restoring sweetness to the day. The tea had spilt and the cup had broken and there was cake here and there by the time it was over, and Beth couldn't remember when things had gone so well. That Lukey.

She'd heard stories of course – she pretended she wasn't listening but she sucked them down for all that – and a lot more was true than them stories let on. Beth sagged against him, loose and moist and smiling.

'Bring ya a new cup next week love,' and his hands patted her naked buttocks.

'Fill ya woodbox too.'

'I'd like that, Lukey.'

***

'Who fixed the door, filled the fuckin woodbox?'

'Oh – Lukey Pease dropped by.' Beth felt herself blushing all over, sweating with it. It was dark, and for once she was glad Leonard had refused to have the electricity.

Leonard grunted.

'See that little terd around here I'll take a pickhandle to 'im.'

'I can't split them ironbark stumps Len.'

Leonard grunted again.

'Split more than ironbark give 'im half a chance – you keep ya fuckin legs shut, hear?'

Beth found herself smiling. Leonard had shown no interest in her legs open or shut for the last fifteen twenty years.

Whereas Lukey –

'What ya grinning like that for?'

'Oh Len – you're so funny is all.'

'Catch ya with that little cockroach ya'll see how funny I am.'

'For goodness sakes Len – he just put the screen door back on its hinges and filled the woodbox. What's wrong with that?'

Leonard rose from his chair slow and deliberate like he did everything, walked around the table to where Beth sat.

He hit the side of her head with a treefeller's hand.

Beth fell over, chair and all,

She watched Len's boots through a red haze as they clumped up the stairs.

You couldn't fool Len.

She should of known better.

He didn't care tuppence about her himself, but there was no mucking around with what was his. Lukey better watch out – she had too, come to that. Beth pushed the chair off her and climbed slowly to uncertain feet. The kitchen had an unsettling spin to it in varying shades of red. Beth let her head hang and her eyes filled with hot lead.

She shook her head, which was a mistake.

Maybe she could sleep in the girls' old room, empty these last ten years.

She crept up the stairs, but he was waiting at the top.

He pointed at the bedroom and Beth walked in and Len followed, locked the door, took the key out and put it in his pocket.

***

Beth couldn't drag herself out of bed to light the stove in the morning – first time in years she hadn't made Len his breakfast. He could eat his oats cold if he wanted oats, get his own lunch, do what he liked. She lay there until she heard the truck grind away down the road before she fell asleep.

Sun on Beth's face woke her – must be ten o'clock but when she peered at the clock on the dresser there were two clocks, foggy brown, and she could not make out the time. Two of everything she discovered and all of them brown. She climbed out of bed and the floor flew up and smacked her in the face. She lay there for a while.

She had to warn Lukey. Lukey spent a large part of his life in the old blue caravan up behind the tip – maybe he was there now. Beth dragged herself across the bedroom, hauled herself up on the banister and stumbled down the stairs.

***

'Jesus Beth!'

For once Lukey was short of wisecracks.

'Len?'

Beth nodded.

'How'd he find out?'

Beth shook her head.

And in that moment something shifted in Lukey Pease's

brain – something solid and heavy clanged into place and the smile faded from his lips.

'Bastard needs teaching a lesson.'

Beth reached for his arm.

'No Lukey, he'll kill you.' But Lukey shrugged her hand away.

'Bastard's got him a lesson coming.'

Lukey loped off down the hill and Beth sat in the doorway of the plywood van watching his scrawny figure work its way down past the tip, dead cars cocking their rusty arses to the sky.

Leonard would kill Lukey. Beth had little doubt Len would take a pickhandle to him – with the pick still on it like as not.

Then he'd come for her. He would, too.

Maybe not kill her – but the time might come when she would hope for that.

Crows flapped heavily in the trees, croaked meaningless carks.

A butcherbird sang its sweet song as if it'd never hung a baby bird on a thorn in its life.

She'd go to the police.

As soon as she thought of that Beth felt better. She hadn't seen much of Sergeant Tom Johnson lately – seen him in church and that – but the Toomeys, like most people up here kept themselves to themselves, and when Tom Johnson drank at the pub, he drank alone.

Unless Mick Dooley was there. Big Mick owned the place and could handle most things, but story was there'd been a time or two when Sergeant Johnson had come in handy.

Mick never let Tom pay for his beer.

Hard men had stripped gold from the creeks and gullies hereabouts a long time back and a few old fossickers still poked around the steep dark hillsides and their secret valleys – came to the pub now and again with a little bag of dust – left without it a week or so later. When the bag was empty – sometimes things happened. Like as not they spent a night or two in the lockup back of the police station after that. There'd been a time Tom paid Beth to bring them meals – but Leonard put a stop to that.

Beth headed down the hill towards the little sandstone police station beside the bridge. There was no sign of Lukey.

She walked under the honeyed stone archway, but the green door was shut, locked. Beth sat on the green wooden bench while the sun slipped down and the cold crept up from the creek.

When the shadows reached where she sat Beth had nowhere else to go.

She rose and headed for home.

***

The chops were hard brown on the plate, the vegetables moulting into the saucepan water and the stove was nearly out, but Leonard was not home.

Beth had cooked bananas and bacon to go with the chops – Len went for bananas and bacon sometimes, scowling at the cost as he ate – but the bananas were dripping through the griddle and the bacon was strips of leather and still no groan and rattle of the old Ford grinding its way up the hill.

Beth walked outside. The night was clear, the stars sharp, frost already settling in the valley. She put another log in the stove and thought of Lukey – his cheeky smile, his busy hands, and in spite of everything she smiled at the memory.

The smile hurt. She was pleased now there were no mirrors in the house, Len didn't go with mirrors. She would not like what they might show her now.

She startled awake in her chair, the stove cold.

No wheel tracks scored the white frost in the yard.

She climbed the stairs to bed.

***

In the morning Beth woke to a house where not a board creaked, not a door rattled, not a plate clinked.

She lay in the bed, watched a window of pale sunlight creep down the bedroom wall. The square of sunlight shimmered, the surface of a pond where some great, shy, speckled trout might slowly rise from secret depths to sip at drifting flies.

In the yard outside a butcher bird sang its heart out.

The woodbox would need filling soon enough.

www.ingramcontent.com/pod-product-compliance
Lightning Source LLC
Chambersburg PA
CBHW050359030726
47503CB00006B/1936